RECKONING
AT RAINDANCE

Other books by Pete Peterson:

The Relentless Gun

RECKONING
AT RAINDANCE

•

Pete Peterson

AVALON BOOKS
NEW YORK

PRINTED IN THE UNITED STATES OF AMERICA
ON ACID-FREE PAPER
BY HADDON CRAFTSMEN, BLOOMSBURG, PENNSYLVANIA

IN MEMORIUM:
To my father, Murl F. Peterson,
by far the finest man I've ever known . . .
and
To his beloved great-grandchildren,
Amanda and Cody Klingbeil.

Chapter One

"Ee-e-e-hah! Hyah! Hyah!"

Whistles and shouts, the whinnies and neighs of sleek horses, the creak of saddle leather, and the slap of lariats on leather chaps were heard on the range and in the breaks of the Dancer Ranch. Jack Dancer's uncle John and a half-dozen vaqueros worked to corral the saddle stock purchased by the JA Ranch of Texas.

Jack Dancer crossed the ranch yard from the barn to the house. As he walked he breathed deeply of the smell of sweet grasses carried on the breeze off the meadow. He looked about him with a warm pride at what had been accomplished in the few years since he and Laura had come to this land on the Gunnison to begin their marriage.

Jack's gun hung idle in a well-worked holster on a peg by the door; a tarnished deputy's badge gathered dust on a shelf above it. They were symbols of a trade he had gladly relinquished to become a rancher, a husband and a father.

John had found the land for the ranch—twelve hundred and eighty acres of prime horse pasture on the banks of the river. In order to purchase the property, the Dancer men had

1

gotten a loan from a Denver bank on the strength of their word, and a handshake for collateral.

Jack and John Dancer were known men, their exploits recounted and embellished around countless campfires throughout the West. Together they had mounted a relentless, prolonged pursuit of four vicious killers, the McCabe brothers. Now, wherever men gathered, their names and deeds were compared with those of Bat Masterson, Temple Houston, Heck Thomas, Bill Hickok and the like. They both sought to avoid the notoriety and acclaim that their epic manhunt had spawned, but it was a tale that demanded telling.

It had begun when young Jack Dancer was in town for a little fun on a Saturday night, but Cash McCabe was looking to add a notch to his gun, and before the night was over, Jack was fleeing for his life with a smoking sixgun in his hand. Frightened and confused, thinking he had killed a man in a forced fight, the gangly farmboy of seventeen escaped onto the dark and lonely Texas plain with the McCabe brothers, sons of a rich carpetbagger, in hot pursuit.

Unable to run Jack to ground, the McCabes sought their revenge by carrying out a brutal attack on his family, inflicting injuries that ultimately led to the deaths of Jack's mother and his brother, Tom.

The McCabe brothers were forced to flee Texas ahead of a storm of outrage over their attack on a woman. They ran to escape justice, but justice followed in the persons of John and Jack Dancer.

The Dancers persevered in the pursuit over hundreds of miles of trails across Texas, New Mexico, Colorado and Wyoming. The weeks and months turned to years. Oftentimes the chase was stalled as the trail was lost to time, wind or weather, but a word dropped in a saloon or a sighting by a drifter would send the Dancers once more to their saddles.

The manhunt was finally ended in an ancient cliff

dwelling when Cash McCabe fell to the relentless gun of Jack Dancer—and the legend was born.

Before Jack and Laura were married, her father, Charlie Tenkiller, worked an unproductive gold claim in the hills above Ouray. The half-breed Cherokee astounded them all when he sold the claim to an eastern consortium for a small fortune. Knowing his own weaknesses, Charlie opted to throw in with the Dancers, investing his unexpected bonanza in the ranch.

"I want to put this here money into the future before I drink it all up. You men run the ranch, I'll put up the capital for development. Three-way partnership, what do you say?"

Even with Charlie's contribution funding necessary purchases, it had not been easy. There had been a barn, the house and outbuildings to raise, corrals and holding pens to put in, a well to be drilled, and a hundred other projects that Jack had not imagined when he and John had first decided on settling here. Jack had wanted Laura to wait in Ouray while he and John got things underway; to allow herself the comfort of a roof over her head, a kitchen in which to cook, and a bed in which to sleep. But his bride would have none of it. She insisted upon sharing in the hardships and the work of the building, reasoning she would share in the benefits and comforts of the dwelling that would be their home. And she wanted, most of all, to be with the man she loved.

As they toiled and built, they set up housekeeping in tents, the four of them. There had been a sleeping tent for Jack and Laura, one for John and Charlie, and an open-sided canopy that served as kitchen and mess tent. They had attacked the work with determination and optimism, each leaning on the others for encouragement and support.

Jack had watched his wife, a town girl all her life, swing a scythe, wield a hammer and a saw, toss a lariat, sit long hours in a saddle, and shoot a rifle to bring down game, adding variety to their indifferent larder. All worked dawn to dusk most days, and Laura was gradually transformed from a refined, seemingly dainty girl into a hardy woman with calluses on the palms of her small hands. Jack suffered to watch her work so hard, but she insisted upon bearing her share of the load.

Initially, they had set up housekeeping in the barn, the first structure to be completed, and Laura did what she could with the sparse resources at her disposal to make it a home. The men had then begun construction of the ranchhouse, a low, rambling collection of five spacious rooms in two sections, connected by a covered dog run.

Once raised and occupied, the house became, and remained, Laura Dancer's domain.

Jack stepped onto the porch and entered the house, letting the screen door slam shut behind him, and walked to a patch of sunlight on the floor beneath a south window. An infant played contentedly on a blanket in the warm sun, raven-black hair glistening in the bright light. His son, Little Tom. Jack bent to reach the baby, a stocky youngster.

"You are your mama's boy, for sure. A little papoose if I ever saw one."

Laura hollered from the kitchen. "You wash up before you start messing with that child."

Jack looked around. How in tarnation could that woman tell what he was up to when she could not see him? It happened constantly, and it never ceased to befuddle him. Ignoring the directive, he hoisted Tommy, holding the smiling baby above his upturned face, catching a string of slobber on the chin for his effort. He shouted out to Laura.

"Nothin' on me that he won't be gettin' used to sooner or later, honey. A little horse manure, maybe . . . but that smells like money to a Dancer."

Laura came into the room, wiping flour from her hands onto her apron.

"You are incorrigible, Jack Dancer." She plucked the baby out of his daddy's arms.

"Rider comin', Jack."

The shout from the yard brought Jack and Laura scurrying to the porch where Charlie stood pointing toward an approaching rider.

"It's a woman, ridin' sidesaddle," Jack reported.

Jack squinted in the bright sun to make out the rider. As recognition lit his face he stepped off the porch onto the hardpack of the yard, Charlie following.

"Why it looks to be Miz Coffee, Sam's wife. What in tarnation is she doin' ridin' out this way all alone?"

Jack and Charlie walked to meet the unexpected visitor. Handing the reins of her mount to Charlie, Jack helped the lady from her saddle.

"How are you, Jack? Hello, Mr. Tenkiller." Her salutations were spoken in a voice shaky with fatigue.

"Miz Coffee . . . is something wrong?" Jack asked, as he escorted the trail-worn woman to the house.

"Yes! I'm saddle-beat and coated with enough Colorado dirt to plant pole beans."

Laura shifted the baby to her left arm, extending her right to assist the visitor to the porch.

"I mean in town," Jack persisted. "Is anything wrong with . . ."

"She knows what you mean, Jack," Laura scolded. "Let the poor woman catch her breath, get in the door and get cleaned up and rested before you jump on her. You aren't wearing a badge, anymore."

Mrs. Coffee stopped at the door to admire the baby.

"My, my, look at you. What a healthy, handsome young 'un. What did you name him, Laura?"

"Tom," Jack volunteered, "after my brother." He was grinning proudly. There was a softness in his eyes, seeing his son smile for company.

Laura thrust the baby at its father, ushering Mrs. Coffee through the door.

"There's fresh washwater in the pitcher on the night stand in the bedroom, Mary Ruth. You wash, lie down and rest for a while, if you like, while I start dinner. Then we'll have us a nice long visit."

Jack trailed his wife around the kitchen as she busied herself. He jostled Tommy in his arms, rhythmically patting the baby's diapered bottom.

"Something *is* wrong, Jack," Laura offered. "She wouldn't have ridden all this way just to see the baby. Sam wouldn't have allowed it."

When Mary Ruth Coffee emerged from the other room, she looked much refreshed. Composed, assured, almost elegant, the way Jack remembered her. Her dress had been carefully brushed free of dust, her hair pulled slickly into a bun at the base of her neck. She smiled weakly.

"Dinner will be ready shortly. Sit here," Laura said, "I've made you a nice cup of tea."

"That will be a refreshing change. Sam is scornful of tea. Says we have a name to live up to," Mrs. Coffee said with a wry smile. She looked around the ranchhouse interior as she seated herself. "You've a fine place here. You all have done much in so short a time. Three years, is it?"

"Two years, seven months and ten days," Laura told her, smiling, "but who's counting?" She turned to Jack, handing him a small, cheesecloth-bundled tidbit. "Take Tommy in, put him in his crib and give him his sugar-tit, will you, Jack . . . and holler at daddy, have him catch up a couple of fryers. Then come back in and join us."

"Yes'm."

Jack and the baby disappeared into the bedroom.

"Well, don't that beat all," Mary Ruth said, watching them go.

As she turned back to face Laura, unsummoned tears began to flow down her cheeks.

Jack returned to the kitchen. Mrs. Coffee, her eyes filled with fear and pain, blurted out, "I need your help, Jack, desperately. Sam is missing."

"It was my fault. I drove him to it."

Mary Ruth told them that Sam Coffee had been missing for almost two weeks. He had left his deputy, Tim Bell, in charge of the office and ridden off in pursuit of a wanted felon, for the reward posted on the man's head.

"That doesn't sound like something Sam would be apt to do," Jack said.

"It wasn't. I'd been on him for months to quit the law, get us a little place somewhere. Even move back East, to Georgia, where my folks are.

"I've always been afraid, him being a lawman. I've patched his hide a thousand times over the years, everything from being cut open to broken bones, missin' teeth and bruises. His jaw has been broken twice, his nose a dozen times. He's got too old for that kind of nonsense, Jack! I lived with the fear he'd be found dead in an alley some Sunday morning, and I told him so, over and over."

"Well, it's no secret that a town marshal doesn't make a lot of money. We've never been able to put more than a few dollars by."

"That's why I say I drove him to it. He's out trying to get the reward money for me, to put toward the day we quit marshalin'."

Mrs. Coffee went on to explain that a broadside had come across Sam's desk on one Buck Turnbull, alias

Blackpowder Buck, wanted in Boulder for robbery and murder. The reward for his capture was fifteen hundred dollars.

"Sam had crossed paths with this Turnbull fellow when he worked the mines. Had him in jail a good many times back then, generally for drunk and disorderly. He remembered some things the man had talked about while he was in custody. Things that made him think he might know where Buck Turnbull was holed up.

"I begged him not to go. I told him the money wasn't important, that I'd sooner he stayed a lawman. But his mind was set and he took out after Turnbull."

Mary Ruth was wringing her hands, and torment was visible in her eyes.

"Jack, you know that Sam is no gunhand. He is a brawler. A good one . . . but that's all. He's likely layin' out there wounded somewhere. He could even be . . ."

She began to sob. Laura moved to slip an arm around her shoulders. Jack placed a comforting hand on her forearm.

"Now, now. Let's not borrow trouble that likely will never happen, Miz Coffee," Jack said. "He could be riding into Boulder now, with this Turnbull in tow. He could even be back in Ouray, waiting for you."

"I wired the marshal in Boulder. He hadn't seen hide nor hair of him. Same for Denver, Telluride, Climax and Leadville.

"I know I shouldn't have come to you folks with this. I–I just didn't know where else to turn."

"You got any notion where Sam figured this man to be hiding?"

Mary Ruth shook her head.

"Not really. North and some west, Sam said. Somewhere in the Sawatch. That's all I know."

"You try not to worry so, Miz Coffee. Sam's a good man, and he's likely all right. We'll figure something out."

The distraught woman pushed to her feet, saying, "If you don't mind, I believe I will lie down and rest awhile. Then I want to be on my way. I want to be there when Sam gets home. You know how he worries."

When Mary Ruth Coffee pushed shut the bedroom door, Laura poured Jack a cup of coffee and sat down opposite him at the table. She leaned forward.

"Jack, you must help that poor woman. You must ride out and find Sam Coffee."

"I wouldn't know where to even start to look, Laura. He could be anywhere. Besides, I don't want to leave you and the baby."

"The baby and I will be just fine. You and John ran down the McCabes with no more to go on. You can find your friend, as well. If you don't think you can find him yourself, take John with you."

"Oh, no. I'm for sure not going to leave you here, defenseless. I'll go, but John stays. Someone has to keep the ranch running, and there's no other man living I'd trust to protect you and Little Tom."

Laura smiled, having gotten the result she had been after all along.

"I appreciate that, Jack, darling . . . though I have never considered myself defenseless. I can't imagine any situation that might arise that we couldn't handle—John, Daddy and me. You go find Sam. Don't worry about us. And hurry back safe to me."

They convinced Mrs. Coffee to stay over until morning, when Jack would drive her back to Ouray in the buckboard.

The previous spring, John had traded with the Nez Perce Indians, in Idaho, for a dozen head of breeding stock from their herd of magnificent spotted horses—appaloosas. He convinced Jack to ride one of the Nez Perce stallions instead of his buckskin, for the appaloosa was mountain-bred, and would be a valuable ally in the wilds of the Sawatch range.

So, with the first gray of false dawn to show them the trail, and saddle horses tied to the tailgate of the wagon, Jack flicked the reins over the rumps of the wagon team, hollering, "Hyah." He was starting for Ouray and a search of indeterminate length and inexact direction—away from all he had helped build, all he held dear in life.

Chapter Two

"What's that off yonder, daughter?"

The Dancer household had finished the evening meal and all were relaxing on the porch, prior to retiring. Charlie Tenkiller squinted as he asked the question. Laura stopped the motion of the chair in which she was rocking the baby and threw a rigid palm to her brow, shading her eyes from the low angle of a setting sun.

"Looks to be a wagon, with a canvas cover."

John leaned away from the post that supported his back, dropped a partially whittled stick in his lap and plucked the odorous pipe from between clenched teeth. He craned his neck in order to observe what had precipitated all the confounded conversation.

"Humph. Movers most likely. Gettin' too all-fired crowded hereabouts for my likin'."

"Been a good many years since I seen a wagon of that sort," Charlie said. "Hope it ain't the start of another danged migration."

"You two mind your language around the baby. I'll go inside and put on a pot of coffee, in case they stop."

The creaking wagon advanced out of the hastening

11

gloom, pulling into the ranchyard. The driver leaned back on the reins as the rickety conveyance drew alongside the porch. "Ho, up, mules."

Upon ascertaining that the wagon was coming to the ranch, John Dancer went for his gunbelt, hanging just inside the door. As he strapped the weapon around his lean hips, he flipped the loop from the cocking piece with his thumb. He stepped off the porch as the wagon stopped.

"Help you folks?"

The cadaverous man gripping the reins shifted the quid in his cheek and spat the brown effluent on the hardpan near John's boot.

"Be obliged if I could water my team, and the poor beasts could use a bait of grain."

The skin around the man's eyes was sunken and discolored, his complexion sallow beneath a heavy cake of trail dirt. His hair and beard hung stiffly in filthy tangles. The woman beside the driver did not look as healthy or as clean as her mate. A frail toddler, a girl, was huddled between them, wrapped in a tattered blanket. She was sobbing quietly and quaking violently. Her tiny, tear-streaked cheeks showed high color beneath the grime, and her eyes were rimmed in red.

John gestured with the toss of a thumb over his left shoulder. "River's not three hundred yards, yonder, and good graze all around, mister."

As John spoke to the stranger's request, Laura returned to the porch.

"Shame on you, John Dancer. Where are your manners?"

"John Dancer?" The driver's jaw dropped. He paled, seeming to shrink. "The West Texas gunman?"

"The rancher, mister."

Then Laura's eyes found the child. She gasped.

"Oh, my. That baby is sick! Please . . . bring her inside."

"Ain't necessary," the man growled. "Just a touch of the catarrh."

"Nonsense," Laura insisted, shifting her gaze to the woman. "The child needs rest, and something hot in her stomach. Won't you come in? Please?"

The pitiful wretch of a woman looked pleadingly at her husband. "Wouldn't hurt, would it, Rufus? Just for a while?"

The man slid off the wagon seat and walked to the mules. "Take her in, then, while I tend these animals."

John tugged at Laura's sleeve.

"I wouldn't take these folks into the house, Laura. Let me put them up in the barn."

"John . . . that child is *sick*."

"All the more reason not to drag them into your home. You got a young 'un of your own to consider."

Charlie nodded his agreement. "You don't know what that little girl might be carryin', honey. Give them some food and let 'em be on their way."

But they were talking to Laura's back. She was reaching to take the ailing toddler from its mother.

After Jack got Sam Coffee's wife home and safely settled in, he drove the buckboard around back, stabled the wagon team and Mary Ruth's pony, then saddled the appaloosa. Not one to walk when he could ride, Dancer mounted and headed for the marshal's office two blocks away.

"Evenin'," he said to the deputy as he moved into the office, "you Tim Bell?"

The young man's answer came in back of a nod. "Yep. And you must be Jack Dancer."

"How do you know me?"

"Saw you ride in with Sam's missus," Bell told him. "But I feel like I ought to know you anyhow. Can't say as I like you much, neither."

Dancer was taken aback. "Oh? I done something to you that I don't know about?"

"Just joshin', Mr. Dancer," Bell said, cracking a smile.

"Sam talks about you a good deal. Always holdin' you up to me . . . Jack Dancer done this, Dancer used to do it thisaway. I come off a poor second most every time."

Jack laughed. "Don't you worry about that. He did the same to me when I was in your boots, comparing my actions to what was done before me."

"I'd heard of you before I pinned this star to my chest, though. How you ran down those . . . McCalls, was it?"

"McCabes."

Bell offered his hand. "Anyhow, I'm proud to meet you. I haven't had a word from Sam, if that's why you're here."

Jack eased into a chair across the desk from the young deputy.

"You know anything about the man he took out after . . . this Buck Turnbull?"

"No more than was on that wanted poster."

"Sam take that with him, or do you still have it?"

"He took that one, but another came in the batch I got off the stage yesterday. Got it right here."

Bell reached into a desk drawer and flipped the sheet across the desk. Dancer read the printed information, learning little more than what Mrs. Coffee had told him, except that the fugitive employed the use of explosives in his crimes. There was no likeness of the outlaw on the notice.

"You going out after Sam, Mr. Dancer?"

"I reckon. But first, I'm going to mosey over to Telluride, see if I can turn up any more about this Turnbull. What was Sam riding when he left out of here? That big buckskin he's partial to?"

Bell nodded and Jack pushed to his feet and shook the deputy's hand.

"Thanks, Bell. You hold the lid on Ouray. I'll go get that knuckleheaded marshal of ours."

Jack succumbed to Mrs. Coffee's offer to stay the night. He was out at dawn, a hearty breakfast holding him in the saddle, headed for Telluride.

Laura swiped at heavy beads of perspiration on her brow with a forearm as she applied a fresh compress to the fevered brow of her son.

"He's worse," she told John in a scratchy voice, "much worse. Can't keep a thing in his stomach, not even water. And he's got the runs, real bad. Maybe you'd better ride for the doctor. There's nothing more I know to do."

"Best that Charlie go," John told her, placing a hand on her shoulder. "I promised Jack I'd look after things here."

"Yes. I'll go," Charlie said. There was the furrowed look of deep concern on the old Indian's face. "Don't you worry, girl. Little Tom is strong. He'll be well again in no time."

"It's my fault." Laura was on the verge of tears. Her fine features were drawn tight with strain and worry. "You warned me, both of you, not to bring those people into my home."

John grasped Laura by the shoulders, pulling her to her feet.

"Nobody faults you for having a good heart. You're tired, Laura. You look to be feeling poorly yourself. You go and rest. I'll watch the boy while Charlie rides for the doctor. Go on, now."

Laura Dancer nodded her compliance, turning toward the bedroom. As she left the room, she said, "Hurry, Daddy. Please hurry."

They heard Laura convulse in a fit of vomiting as John moved to the front door. "Stay with Little Tom, my old friend, while I saddle your horse. I got a bad feeling that we are running out of time."

* * *

The half-breed Comanche called Stone Wolf slid off the side of his limping pony and bent to examine the horse's injured foreleg. Rising again, he sighed, then reached to the knife at his belt. The anger he felt was visible only in the depths of his black eyes.

He unsaddled the piebald horse and stashed his gear to one side. Stepping then to the animal's head, Stone Wolf used his knife to deftly end its misery, and watched as it crumpled in a lifeless heap.

Stone Wolf wore a fur vest over his brick-colored, lean-muscled bare torso, along with fringed leather britches and boot-high moccasins. His dead black eyes were empty wells set deep under the glowering brow of a hawk-like face, chiseled roughly from the granite hardness of his heritage. His glistening black hair hung straight to the small of his back, encircled at the brow by a bright red headband of twisted cloth. The man was a warrior.

Taking up his rifle and saddlebags, Stone Wolf made his way to the lip of a nearby ledge that afforded a view of the landscape for miles in every direction. He checked the load in the weapon, then settled into a comfortable position against a rock. Drawing a chunk of jerked venison from a saddlebag, he popped it into his mouth, chewing thoughtfully. Settling the long gun across his lap, Stone Wolf waited.

Charlie Tenkiller bent low in the saddle, urging the roan to go faster with sharp jabs of his heels. The game mustang was lathered and blowing, but it did not falter. It was but a season removed from running free on the range, and John Dancer had chosen the animal for its endurance.

From his vantage point above the trail, Stone Wolf spied the rushing rider.

"That fool is going to kill my horse." He raised the rifle to his shoulder, his practiced eye leading the target without conscious calculation. Stone Wolf fired.

A mighty blow from an unseen force struck Charlie in the side, lifting him abruptly from the saddle and slamming him to the turf. Not until he had tumbled to a halt did Cherokee Charlie hear the sound of the shot that had downed him. His eyes followed the path of pain to the ugly wound that the bullet had made, and he saw the gush of dark blood.

Charlie raised his head, surveying his surroundings for his horse, and for the sniper. The roan had stopped a few hundred yards down the trail and was dancing nervously. Charlie slapped his thigh, cursing himself for leaving home without a sidearm. His rifle was resting in the scabbard on his saddle, inaccessible. From the corner of his eye, he caught movement. A dark figure was advancing at a leisurely lope, across the flat toward the standing horse, a rifle dangling at the end of his arm.

Stone Wolf approached the skittish mustang slowly, making soft sounds, his arm extended to capture the hanging reins of the harness. With the reins in hand, the Indian spoke soothingly to his new mount, rubbing its muzzle, caressing its neck. He leaped to the saddle in a vault and guided the mustang back down the trail toward his victim.

He looked down on the bleeding form of Charlie Tenkiller. "Humph. Cherokee." Stone Wolf spat out the word.

Charlie looked into his attacker's impassive face and knew that he was about to die.

"Please, mister. Take the horse, but you got to ride on into town for the doctor. My grandson is bad sick, and I'm feared my daughter has caught it too. They'll die without help soon. I'll tell you where to send him."

Stone Wolf raised the barrel of the rifle in his hand.

"You have no more time for talk."

The report of the shot that killed Charlie Tenkiller was swallowed in empty space, with none to hear but his executioner.

* * *

Armed with fresh information, Jack Dancer pushed the appaloosa up the trail toward Climax. He wasted no time, for he was anxious to find his friend, and to return home, to his wife and son.

Jack had inquired at the offices of several mining companies in Telluride, seeking information on Buck Turnbull, all to no avail. Then he had made the rounds of the mining camps, talking to individuals that might have known the man. One Cousin Jack remembered Turnbull as a tough and a bully, who would slit his best friend's throat over a drink or a woman, but he had no knowledge of the man's habits or his whereabouts.

"Know one bloke that might," the miner had said, "name of Culligan. He was residing in a jail cell in town, last I heard."

Jack scolded himself on the way back to town for not having checked with the local law in the beginning. Culligan was, indeed, incarcerated, but was not inclined to discuss Turnbull, fearing the consequences should the man learn of it. It was only after Jack agreed to post his bond that he revealed that the fugitive had deserted a cabin in the wilds of the Sawatch, south and west of Climax, to work the mines of Telluride. "That was years back," Culligan said, "and he mightn't be there now, but it's the only guess I got."

So Jack had struck out, once again on the hunt for a killer. As he rode, his senses reverted to those of the hunter. He could not expect to raise a physical trail after so long a time, but he could place himself in the mind of his quarry—in this instance, a friend, a man he knew well.

Jack was painfully aware that, if Sam Coffee was dead, he might never discover what had happened to him. Many daring men had disappeared in the wilderness, never to be heard from. Their weathered bones lay scattered in the myr-

iad parks and forests and rivers of the Rockies. Their histo-
ries would forever remain unwritten. The hunter rode the
lonely trail with caution, for he did not wish to join their
ranks. Dancer wandered the slopes and gullies of the area
south of Climax for days, searching for Turnbull's cabin, to
no good end.

As Jack broke camp, despair rode his shoulders. He had
found no sign of human habitation let alone any structure
that he could attach to the outlaw, Blackpowder Buck.

Suddenly, the sound of a large animal crashing through
the brush sent Jack diving for the bushes, gun drawn and
cocked. A horse wandered into the camp, hungry for human
companionship. A big, saddled buckskin. *Sam Coffee's
horse!*

Dancer bounded from cover, holstering his drawn pistol,
catching the dragging reins of the marshal's pet mount.

"Sandy, ol' boy. Where's your two-legged partner? Can
you tell me?"

Jack figured that it probably could. He could backtrack
the horse to the point where Sam had lost control of it, by
whatever circumstance, and, hopefully, he would find Sam
Coffee there. He checked the buckskin's legs and withers,
then the saddle on it's back. Sam's rifle was missing from
the boot. There was no sign of blood. The horse had traveled
a good ways, fording a creek at some point, for there was
dried mud from the hooves to above the fetlocks. He patted
the horse's neck, then fed it a bait of grain from a sack tied
to Sam's saddle.

Mounted on the appaloosa and trailing the buckskin on a
lead, Jack struck out, eyes on the trail left by the loose horse
of Marshal Sam Coffee.

Dancer sent a silent prayer skyward.

Please, Lord, let that rascal be alive.

* * *

As Jack cleared the tree line at the edge of a meadow, the buckskin balked, pulling violently against its lead. The horse reared, wild-eyed, nostrils flaring.

"What's the trouble, boy?"

Dancer retreated immediately, back into the thick cover of the evergreens, heeding the warning that the animal had so dramatically delivered. He tethered the horses well back in the trees, drew his rifle from the saddle boot and crept back to the clearing.

The day was bright, just a few high, wind-tattered clouds showing against the deep blue of the sky. Birds of varied feather went noisily about the business of making a living, showing no signs of alarm. Jack saw nothing upon the meadow grasses to pose a threat. Still, the horse had not panicked needlessly. He waited.

The park stretched before him in verdant splendor, ending abruptly at the base of a steep bluff, a quarter of a mile distant. What was that in the cliff? A cave? The opening of a mine shaft? He could not make it out. Shuffling back through a heavy undergrowth of lush ferns to the horses, Dancer dug into his saddlebags, coming out with a mariner's glass. He hurried back to his post at the edge of the wood.

Raising the glass to his eye, he adjusted the telescoping lens to focus on the opening in the black bluff. A mine. Abandoned, by the look of it. Jack eased back on his haunches to ponder his next move. He could perceive no danger ahead of him. Perhaps Coffee's mount was reacting to something that had happened here.

Leaving the buckskin tethered in the trees, Dancer advanced onto the meadow, rifle across the bow of his saddle. He was following what remained of the faint backtrail of Coffee's horse. Sure enough, it was leading him directly toward the yawning, black opening in the mountainside. Jack pulled back the cocking piece of the Henry rifle.

The fading tracks of the buckskin led him to a small copse

of aspen, a hundred yards to the right of the mouth of the mine. Examining the churned earth beneath a tall aspen, Jack determined that Sam had tethered his horse to the pale trunk, then gone on afoot, undoubtedly to the mine. Something must have happened to Coffee then, for after being left a long while, the horse had loosened its tether. Might have gotten thirsty. Maybe frightened. By what? Dancer saw no sign of animal threat, no print of cat or grizzly. If the buckskin was scared off, the thing that frightened it had been man-made.

Dancer tied the appaloosa to the same aspen, checked the loads in pistol and rifle, and advanced toward the cavernous opening of the abandoned mine.

Reading the footprints in the earth before the entrance, Jack was able to determine that, as recently as a few days past, two different men had entered the excavation; one man wearing riding boots, the other shod in brogans with flat soles. There was a thin trail of black ash leading into the tunnel. A fuse? There were indications that the fellow in brogans had come and gone from the mine repeatedly. The boot prints led *in* only. Sam Coffee, or what was left of him, was in that black hole!

Jack advanced a few feet into the tunnel. He struck a match, holding it above his head, searching for a lantern, a candle, a torch. He found a long stick, the end wrapped in blackened cloth. He sniffed it, detecting the strong odor of coal oil.

Dancer brought the torch to life and began a slow and hesitant descent into the bowels of the mountain.

Chapter Three

John Dancer used the shovel in his callused hands to pound the simple wooden cross into the small mound of earth that covered the grave of Little Tom Dancer. A tear traversed his rugged cheek as he turned his face to the sky, bellowing out his rage.

How on God's earth am I goin' to break all this to Jack? he asked himself. John felt a heavy burden of guilt, a burden that threatened to crush his spirit. His nephew and partner, the person that John loved more than any other, had depended upon him to keep his little family safe in his absence, and he had failed. He felt guilty that he, himself, had not caught the disease. He felt that he should have driven those filthy movers off the ranch the moment he caught their sickly odor. Killed them if necessary. Instead, he had let pretty little Laura buffalo him; let her override his caution with her Samaritan goodness.

Now Laura was gone too. Buried beside her son. Two hastily fashioned crosses on a lonely rise of ground overlooking the river—two wooden crosses marking the sum of Jack Dancer's world. At that instant, John would have gladly crawled into his own grave if the two happy young souls he had buried here could rise and laugh again.

John got to his feet, not having realized that he had fallen to his knees. He moved as in a daze toward the barn. He must ride out to find what had happened to Charlie, gone now for five days. Perhaps, after taking to the trail, the old Indian had also fallen victim to the pestilence. Something was mighty wrong, for neither Charlie nor the doctor he was riding to fetch had appeared back at the ranch.

John saddled the black, moving from habit rather than motivation, swung into leather and looked once again toward the graves of Laura and her baby. He rode from the ranch on the trail taken lifetimes ago by Charlie Tenkiller.

As he rode, the West Texas gunman noted that a man's trail looks mighty bleary when viewed through a curtain of tears.

The chilling sight of buzzards circling against a blue-steel sky, before swooping to a ghoulish banquet on the valley floor, drew John Dancer like a magnet. He put spurs to the black, hoping that a deer, a bear, anything with four legs, was the carrion attracting Nature's housekeepers—but he sensed that he was likely riding toward the remains of Cherokee Charlie Tenkiller.

John's spirit lifted as he spied the carcass of a pie-bald pony. Coyotes, buzzards and magpies were queued up, all vying for places at the table. John drew his sixgun, firing in the air to scatter the scavengers. He rode to the partially devoured carcass. Not enough of it left to tell what had befallen the beast. The ground around the bloody leavings of the horse was busy with the prints of the diners, so John circled the site, searching for tracks of a rider. There. Moccasins. Leading toward a sharp rise in the flat landscape. He advanced at a trot to the spot where Stone Wolf had awaited a victim of convenience.

The plot of the tragic story played out for John Dancer as he followed the tracks that the Indian had left upon the ground. He saw where Stone Wolf had caught up to the riderless mustang, then followed the horse's hoofprints to the spot where Charlie had lain, helpless to defend himself against the savage renegade looming over him.

There was not enough remaining of the old Indian to continue to draw scavengers. The stripped bones of his skeleton were scattered over a wide area.

John saw where Charlie's killer had stopped his horse. Saw the black stain on the earth where Charlie's life had spilled forth. *All to give some lousy drygulcher a ride!*

Shaken and weary, John slipped from the saddle and began methodically to gather the bones of a friend. He buried them there, where Charlie Tenkiller had died.

When he was done, filled with a building rage, John looked around, wanting to kill something—but no living thing appeared as volunteer.

He mounted then, a man swamped by the shroud of death that surrounded him, engulfing him. He must ride to town to speak with the doctor, to describe what had happened at the ranch in hopes the medical man could identify the deadly and invisible specter that had slain his innocent charges. Jack would want to know. Afterward, he would trail the drygulcher that had killed poor Charlie for a horse.

Then, he would go home. He would wait. Wait to do the hardest thing he was ever to do, in this life or any other.

He would tell Jack Dancer that his family was gone.

Dancer figured he had walked a couple hundred yards along the stone passageway when he found his progress blocked by a jumble of rocks. A cave–in, and Jack knew where he would find Sam Coffee. Sam had entered the mine, doubtless looking for Turnbull. Then the vicious fugitive had blown the tunnel in on top of him. Nothing to do but dig out the body and haul it home to Ouray for a proper burial.

Jack had seen an old wheelbarrow about halfway down the passageway. If it was serviceable, it would lighten and speed his grisly chore. He walked back to fetch it, then set about clearing away the rubble, having no guess as to how monumental the undertaking might prove to be.

He had returned for his fourth barrow–load when Jack thought he heard a noise. He stood quietly, listening. Yes. There it was again. A feeble scratching sound. Probably a rat or some other varmint trapped by the slide. And yet, just maybe! Jack scrambled and slipped in his rush to scale the rock heap. He began hurling the heavy chunks of quartz debris to the tunnel floor behind him. After an hour of grueling labor, his arms and shoulders afire from fatigue, Jack could see black space on the other side of the blockage. He wearily worked his way back down the pile, snatched up the torch and climbed back to the opening. Stretching the length of his body, he thrust the light through the gap. He craned his neck to peer into the void on the other side.

"Who–who's there?" The voice was weak, but it was definitely that of Sam Coffee.

"It's me . . . Jack Dancer." His voice echoed through the chamber.

"Jack . . . what are you doing here?"

"Well, Sam, if this is a bad time, I can come back later."

"The crafty rascal suckered me, Jack. I strutted right into that tunnel to drag him out by the neck. He must have hidden in a depression until I passed, for the next thing I knew I heard his footfalls running for the entrance. I wheeled around to follow, then all hell broke loose. When she blew, I was so close to the charge I was thrown off my feet, which probably saved my bacon."

Jack was putting the finishing touches on a splint for Sam's broken right arm, the last of many repairs he had made on the bruised and battered lawman.

"How long you been in there?"

"Can't say for sure, Jack. It's nigh impossible to keep track of time when it's pitch black all around. Three or four days, probably, though it seemed a lifetime.

"If it weren't for you, my friend, that's exactly what it would have been."

Dancer tied the final knot and patted Coffee on the leg to signify that he had finished.

"Nothing any fearless, master woodsman couldn't have pulled off . . .

"I hope to heaven you're done with this bounty-huntin' business, Sam. You sure aren't cut out for it."

"Just help me on that horse. Once I get home, you won't see me outside the town limits without an army with me."

As they rode down the main street of Ouray, a boisterous gaggle of townsfolk began to fall in behind the horses. Mary Ruth Coffee heard the commotion and hurried to the front gate, craning her neck, peering expectantly down the dusty thoroughfare. When she recognized the buckskin, the southern belle of genteel upbringing vaulted over the fence, gathered her skirts in her hands and ran down the street toward her man, tears of joy and relief blurring her way.

Jack sat the appaloosa, smiling as he watched the heartwarming reunion. Suddenly, he was very lonely. He said his good-byes and turned the nose of the spotted stallion toward the trail that led to the Gunnison.

Jack Dancer was going home.

The wind wailed and moaned in the uppermost branches of the aspen, its breath thick with the chill of an early frost. Brittle, golden leaves chattered like teeth in the cold, deserting their lofty homes to huddle in heaps upon the ground against the white trunks and in the cracks and crevices of the forest. It was a time for death, and a time for wailing. It was a time for good-byes and for remembering sunny days now gone.

Jack Dancer sat between the two dark mounds of cold earth that covered the graves of his wife and son. His forehead rested heavily upon arms crossed on raised knees, and he stared without seeing at the ground between his feet. His jaw was shaggy with a week's growth of beard, and he sat unmindful of the bite in the air or of the wind howling in the trees. The fury inside him had cooled, leaving only a hollow where memories echoed off the walls of his soul.

Raising his head to gaze at the charred ruin of the ranch-house, he heard John say again the evil word. "Cholera." The doctor had made a postmortem diagnosis of the dead from John's tear-choked description and had told him to burn the house, to destroy by fire the fiendish phantom that could kill so quickly, without warning and with no regard for guilt or innocence. The blackened rubble of the home Jack had shared with Laura and Little Tom had cooled. The pungent odor of the ashes and the dead surrounded him still.

Jack saw the faces of his dead loves, his wife, his happy infant son. He could not drive away the painful, choking knot that had taken up residence in the base of his throat.

He was tormented by guilt and self-blame. If he had not ridden away, gone off to rescue a fool off chasing rainbows, things might have happened differently—or he, too, might have been struck down by the sickness, dead, but with his loved ones. Oh, Lord! Had he kissed the baby before he left? Had he told Laura how much he loved her? A man gets so accustomed to his treasures, he often forgets to cherish them as he should. Jack did not know how to deal with the suffocating grief or the gnawing guilt.

Jack knew that he should reach out to John, to assure him that he was not to blame. That most loyal of friends, that most blameless of men, felt somehow responsible for the tragedy. But Jack had not even been able to do that. He felt immobilized and useless. Completely without purpose.

Remembering Laura's compassion and courage, Jack forced himself to his feet, abashed at having demonstrated less selflessness than the woman he had loved. He would talk to John, try to convince him that nothing he could have done would have prevented the loss they both suffered so greatly.

He must pull himself together and get on with the business of living, no matter how dreary that prospect might seem at the moment.

Jack tried for weeks to bury his grief in hard work. The Dancer men rolled out each day before dawn to set about rebuilding the ranchhouse. It was to be a smaller, more rustic dwelling this time, as there was no woman, no youngster to consider. They worked the herd, mended fences, cleared brush and broke wild ponies to harness and saddle. Still, Jack was uneasy—restless, irritable and discontent. He would ride alone into the forest, wandering aimlessly, compelled to be on the move for the sake of motion alone.

One morning at breakfast, Jack looked up to find John staring at him, a concerned expression lining his face.

"What?"

"Jack, boy . . . why don't you take off for a while. See some country. There's times a man's got to be on his own to find the peace he's lookin' for. Lord knows, I done my share of roaming when I was your age."

"But, John . . . the ranch. This isn't a one-man operation we got here. I can't put that load on you."

John Dancer waved off his nephew's concern.

"Don't fret about that. If I see I need any help, I can always hire a hand or two. The ranch is doing well, and we still got more'n half of Charlie's investment money in the bank at Denver."

John tossed a thick packet into Jack's lap.

"Travelin' money. Write if you run low. And, Jack . . . son . . . come back as soon as you're ready."

Jack Dancer got to his feet. He placed a palm on John's shoulder as his eyes filled with tears. He could not speak.

Turning, he walked to a corner of the one-room house and began to gather his trail gear. John walked to stand beside him. Reaching to his belt, he pulled out a pistol, reversing it and handing it to Jack, butt first.

"Better take this along. It's a mate to the one you carry now. Never hurts to have an extra in your saddlebags when you are alone on the trail in strange country."

Jack stuck the gun in his belt. Then, on impulse, he threw his arms around his uncle. "Thanks."

John cleared his throat and walked away.

Jack had grown fond of the appaloosa that he had ridden to find Sam Coffee, and he saddled it for the trail. He looked around the ranchyard. John was right. He could not stay here now. Too many ghosts. Too many regrets. He stepped into the saddle and jabbed heels to the spotted stallion, heading east. He had no agenda but to move, and keep moving.

Dancer roamed the mountains for weeks, avoiding towns and settlements, seeking the solitude available to him in the cathedral quiet of the green forests and along the river's run.

Sitting one day on the rim of a great canyon, a cup of steaming coffee in his hand, it occurred to Jack that while there are things in life that are beyond the control of any man, such as the sickness that had come from nowhere to claim his family, some are not. For some trespasses, a price should be extracted. Must be demanded. From men like the elusive savage that had murdered poor Charlie. From men like Turnbull, who killed the innocent to possess what they had not earned.

What was it that Laura had said to him as he left with Mrs. Coffee? *You and John ran down the McCabes. You can find him.*

He *did* have skills he could use for good. He could seek out and bring to justice men that preyed upon their fellow man, for greed, for lust or simply for the sake of evil.

Sprinkling the dregs of his coffee on the dying fire, Jack Dancer began to break camp. He would ride to Ouray, to speak with Marshal Sam Coffee.

Two years had passed since he had collected his first bounty, on Buck Turnbull. Now, the list of felons breaking rock or fertilizing greenery as a result of facing Jack Dancer's relentless gun was long. Dancer had become a name to be feared by men who rode the outlaw trail. He often worked at the commission of agencies of the government or the law, often directly for concerns or individuals that had been victimized by the criminals he pursued.

Jack returned to the ranch on occasion, staying on a while. But the urge to be in the saddle and moving would seize him once more, and he would take to the high country.

He thought often of Laura. But, as time passed, he found it more and more difficult to see her face in his mind. When that occurred, it would leave him feeling guilty and depressed.

One night, after such an episode, Laura came to him in a dream. He saw her face in perfect detail, and she spoke to him.

"Jack, my darling, you know how deeply I loved you. I love you still. But I am at peace here, with Little Tom. Love surrounds us.

"I release you, my dearest, and you must release me and our baby. You must let go of your grief and your bitterness and find your peace.

"Make a new life for yourself. We will have our lost time together, by and by."

When Jack awoke the next morning, he was possessed of an inner peace which he had never known. As he eased into the saddle, he was filled with energy and optimism. With a nudge of a boot heel, he started his horse, riding toward a rising sun.

Chapter Four

The hastily scrawled sign tacked to the warped and weathered siding of the Golconda Saloon declared:

BAR CLOSED TILL
TRILE IS OVER

The yellow daylight of a late afternoon sun forced its way through the grimy panes of the barroom window, skipping over the unkempt heads of a smattering of spectators and directly into the squinting eyes of Judge Amos P. Handy. The judge was seated at a faded, timeworn poker table near the foot of the stairs. He scooted his chair noisily to one side to escape the glare.

The gallery was composed primarily of idle men filling an empty afternoon with other folks' problems, for there was little else to do when the liquor ceased flowing in this after-thought of a town called Raindance. They fidgeted on makeshift benches of long planks supported on kegs, wait-ing impatiently to a man for the machinations of the trial to grind down so that they could get on with the drinking and

32

gambling for which they had come. Four young women of negotiable virtue, habitues of the saloon's second floor, were taking advantage of the potential profitability in the assembly by standing at the bar in commercial advertisement.

Sheriff Harley Brock shifted his booted feet. He was a hulking, dull-looking man with close-set eyes under nonexistent brows. A nose that resembled a fresh-peeled turnip dominated the ruddy slab of his face. His faded red, too-tight shirt clung unbuttoned halfway to his waist, revealing an excess of curly blond hair, now matted and stuck to his chest by rivulets of sweat. The dark circular stains hanging under his arms offered further evidence of the heat and closeness of the cramped saloon's interior. A homemade star was pinned to the lawman's left breast as a semi-apologetic declaration of authority.

Sheriff Brock clenched the manacles of his prisoner in a meaty fist as big as a nail keg. At irregular intervals he inspected the chain that connected the wrist bands, as if fearing his sweaty palm might weaken its links.

The defendant stood straight and tall, his handsome features calm but grim. His black shirt and black denims were neat, but dusty. The toes of his black boots, rubbed free of dust on the backs of his pant legs, glistened brightly, out of place in the dour and shoddy atmosphere of the court. A gunbelt and empty tied-down scabbard hung too lightly around his waist, making him feel naked and ill at ease. He occasionally bent his head from one broad shoulder to the other to scratch at the two-day growth of ash-blond beard that covered the firm set of his jaw. Each time he did so, his captor flinched and studied the chain on the manacles. The prisoner's bearing transmitted the impression of a cougar poised to spring, and there was nothing to the man but rawhide and iron.

Judge Handy, a slight, severe little man with a face carved from flint, stared out with yellowed, weasel-like eyes at the gathered participants in this hastily considered proceeding. He was decked out in a moth-eaten broadcloth coat of faded black, frayed badly at collar and cuffs. Wispy hair the color of wet sand was combed straight forward to cover the telltale pink of a high-rising, balding brow. A collarless, once-white muslin shirt was carelessly tucked into gray, pinstriped high-water trousers that were held on his scant frame by black galluses. Badly scuffed work boots, innocent of polish, completed his wardrobe this day. A patchy stubble of graying beard covered his jowls, a tobacco-stained mustache hung limply from his upper lip, gnawed by a set of mail-order teeth that clacked when he spoke. The judge cleared his throat and, in a voice that could worm a cat, began to deliver his verdict.

"Jack Dancer, if that's your true name, you come riding into Raindance, bold as a bear in a berry patch, with another man's horse in tow, and blood on the saddle. Fact. There ain't a body in town don't know that horse by sight . . . nor know that Rad Macklin, the gent that left out of here on that self-same horse, was totin' a heavy poke, off to buy breedin' stock. Fact."

An ominous muttering passed through the squirming, fidgeting spectators. The stone-faced judge continued, pointing a bony finger with a cracked and dirty nail at the defendant as if it was loaded.

"Once caught, you offer up the lame story that you, a stranger, just happened on the horse down by the crick, and being a good neighbor, brung him in.

"Now I ain't a narrow-minded man. I reckon it could've happened just that way, but . . ."

Handy paused dramatically, enjoying the unaccustomed power of judgeship and the rapt attention of his audience.

"First rattle out of the box you up and slap down a fresh-out-of-the-mint gold piece to pay for a meal. Our banker,

Jim Wheeler here, allows as how Macklin was carrying just such gold coins as that to make his cattle buy. And Macklin's saddlebags is missing, his poke with them.

"Your rifle, sir, had been fired since it was cleaned. You carry a shovel in your packs, real handy-like.

"It don't look good for you, Mr. Dancer. Sure don't."

"Get it done, Handy," an irritated voice urged from behind the bar. "I'm losin' money whilst you're jawin' back over covered ground."

The judge whipped his head around, giving the bartender a withering stare.

"You keep shut, Mulroney. I seldom get the chance to do judgin' on anythin' more than just a rowdy drunk or a wife-beater, and we're gonna do this proper."

The big, surly Irishman behind the bar hawked and spat contemptuously, missing a tarnished brass cuspidor by a good six inches. The judge haughtily turned his attention back to the prisoner.

"Mr. Dancer. You asked the sheriff to send a wire to Marshal Sam Coffee, over to Ouray, saying he could vouch for you. Is that right?"

The defendant nodded. "Yes, sir. Like I told you, I took in a pair of bandits wanted by Wells Fargo. The marshal's got them in the lockup. I was paid in gold coin."

"Now boy, did you see any wires nor poles as you come into town? We got no telegraph. And in my book, a bounty hunter and a killer is birds of a feather."

"You got the wrong bird book, then, Judge," Dancer insisted. "I never killed a man wasn't trying to kill me first!"

"The prisoner will speak when spoke to. I suspicion you figured to stall for time, to stir matters up," Handy said, testily. "Make us small town officials look the fool.

"You got no papers on you saying who you are or where

you're from, but you carry a mighty heavy purse for a man on the trail.

"You ride in with a tied-down gun, on a horse I never seen the likes of in these parts. A fine horse such as could likely outstep any posse in the country . . . claiming to be just passing through. A traveling man.

"By cracky, boy, I know a gun ranny when I see one." Not having a gavel, Judge Handy slammed an empty beer mug hard down on the frayed felt surface of the table.

"Guilty! Guilty as sin of murderin' poor Rad Macklin, disposing of his body and stealing his horse and his gold. Guilty, too, of mistaking us for a passel of fools.

"There's a message I'm sending today to all your kind, men packing trouble on their hips. Ride clear of Raindance, or pay the price . . . and Dancer, you're elected messenger.

"We'll have the hanging in the mornin'."

"Judge, hold on!" Dancer lurched forward, pulled up short by the burly sheriff's grip on the chain of the handcuffs. "You don't even know for sure that man is dead.

"I buried no one. I saw no body. Check with Marshal Coffee, or with Wells Fargo in Denver. At least send out a party to find out what happened. Please!"

"Court's a–journed. Bar's open."

A chorus of whoops erupted as the dozen or so eager spectators sprang to their feet and rushed headlong toward the bar, knocking over the makeshift gallery of benches and jostling the manacled prisoner hard against the sheriff, nearly sending them both to the floor.

Swiftly, his captor off balance, Jack Dancer slipped the gun from the lawman's holster, shoved him roughly to the sawdust–covered floor and immediately bolted for the door. Turning at the entry he raised the pistol, fired, then watched as the crude coal oil lamp fixture, its supporting rope severed cleanly by the bullet, fell from the ceiling to the plank floor, shattering and showering the startled judge and the still-prone, sawdust-spitting sheriff with glass and fuel.

Judge Handy dashed quickly under the stairwell, yowling like a gut-shot panther. Ready and anxious to send a hapless stranger to the gallows on flimsy evidence, the backwoods magistrate was not ready to die.

"First man to poke his head through this door," Dancer warned over his shoulder, "gets a new blue eye."

Several horses stood hitched at the timeworn rail in front of the saloon, now prancing nervously, straining at their tethers. Not figuring to risk the time to liberate his own horse from the livery, Dancer instantly evaluated the available mounts, picking a likely looking zebra dun. He sprang to the saddle, pausing to throw another shot at the saloon, dusting back a few of the incautious occupants peeking over the scabbed and peeling tops of the batwing doors. Then, having unhitched the other saddled mounts at the rail, he took off along the rutted street, driving the small, liberated herd of horses before him.

Hearing a chorus of curses, shouts and epithets, Dancer turned to look back on the confused, frustrated mob milling in the dirt street, shaking their fists and slamming their hats to the ground.

Jack Dancer waved with manacled hands as he disappeared over the rise that led out of town.

There had been a half-hearted pursuit from a few townsmen, but the escaped prisoner easily eluded them in the thickly forested hillsides surrounding the town. Now he watched from a vantage point high above the cluster of buildings and shacks as the last flickering lamp was extinguished in the dark streets of Raindance.

As he studied the structures below, Jack could almost feel the raspy touch and smell the dead-hay odor of hemp around his neck. He shuddered.

Dancer sat on his haunches, absently chewing on a leathery piece of jerked beef he had found in the saddlebags on the dun. He determined that he must discover what had actually happened to the Macklin hombre to prove himself innocent of any wrongdoing.

It would be simpler just to ride away, of course, but he did not want to spend his future watching his backtrail. He was a man that valued his freedom of movement, and he valued his good name, such as it was. He wanted no rewards offered, no dodgers out on Jack Dancer.

All right then, first things first. He must get the manacles off his wrists. He wanted his own guns—a matched pair of Colt Peacemaker .44 revolvers, a Henry repeating rifle, and a ten-gauge Greener shotgun. He wanted to recover his fine appaloosa stud, his pack horse and the rest of his gear. And he wanted, maybe worst of all, a cup of strong, hot coffee.

Well, all of those things were there, in those darkened buildings far below. That sour-smelling baboon of a sheriff had the key to the cuffs and probably had his guns. Just sitting by seemed worse than doing, so Dancer stood up, stretched, hitched up his britches and swung into leather.

The journey that had led him to this fix had started as a pleasure trip.

Dancer had helped settle a range war in Montana, between a group of small ranchers and a cattle baron, named Henry Frost. Settled it in Sam Colt's court of Western justice, where all verdicts are final. Frost and several of his hired guns had taken up permanent residency in Miles City's Boot Hill when the gunsmoke cleared, and the rest of the crew had decided on location to a gentler climate.

Instead of heading back to the ranch in Colorado, Jack had decided to visit his friends, Smoke and Long Bill, who were punchers on Major Amos Warfield's ranch Wyoming, south of Cheyenne. The major wanted Jack to hire on for a spell, but spending twelve or fourteen hours a day chasing half–wild longhorns out of brush-choked gullies while forking the hurricane deck of a broomtail mustang had lost its fascination for Dancer. So, after a visit of a few days, he struck out again for the Gunnison, and home.

He had elected to travel a roundabout course in order to take in a part of the country he had never ridden through. That was how he had stumbled into the missing man's horse outside of Raindance, and into the threat of a hangman's noose.

The tall man in black, stealing his way under cover of darkness toward Raindance, was becoming known throughout the West as a mean man with a gun, and a hunter of men.

Now, Jack Dancer was the hunted.

He tied the zebra dun to a low bush on the outskirts of town, then melded into the dark shadows at the weather–beaten side of the nearest structure, a house of pleasure. Hearing no sound, save the whistling snore of one of the trollops sleeping inside, Dancer rounded the corner and crept furtively along the backs of buildings until he reached what he believed to be the sheriff's office and quarters.

The rear door was kept locked and barred, he remembered. A window, the missing lower pane replaced by an oiled cloth, was raised to allow for ventilation. Dancer stood listening for a long moment, then, pulling the sheriff's borrowed pistol from his belt, he slowly raised the window to a height that would allow access. He paused to listen again, hearing no sounds but those of the night. The manacled intruder scrambled swiftly and silently through the opening, taking special pains not to rattle the chain that bound his wrists.

Once inside, Dancer stood, motionless and silent, allowing his eyes to adjust to the darker blackness of the room. He was in a small storeroom where he had been held overnight awaiting trial. The town had no jail, no cell, so the sheriff kept his occasional prisoners here, chained to the rustic shelving that filled the south wall.

Dancer stepped gingerly across the filthy blankets of the pallet that served as a bed, thankful that no prisoner now occupied the room. The door had been padlocked when he had been held here. He hoped that was not the case now.

He carefully turned the chipped porcelain knob, the door yielded to his pressure, and he stole soundlessly into the front room that served as office and sleeping quarters for Harley Brock. The inert form of the sheriff loomed black and mountainous on the cot against the far wall. Dancer crossed the room, pausing once at the creaking of a loose floor board, to the battered desk. Finding matches in the top drawer, he lifted the chimney of the coal oil lamp to light the wick. The flame sputtered and caught, bathing the room in pale yellow light.

The hulking, blanketed form on the cot stirred momentarily, then settled back into the heavy, even breathing of deep sleep. Dancer searched the desk top and the two drawers for the keys to his chains. Finding nothing, he moved the lamp to rest on a three-legged stool beside the cot. He prodded the sleeping figure with the cold, hard barrel of the pistol.

"Morning, Sheriff Brock," Dancer whispered.

Slowly the sheriff came awake, grinding the heels of his hands into his eyes. Abruptly, recognition dawned.

"Wha . . . you!"

"Shhh," Dancer cautioned, brandishing the sheriff's pistol under his bulbous nose. He held out the manacles.

"The key, if you will."

Brock slapped in reflex at his chest pocket. "Blamed if I will," he whispered, "I . . ."

Dancer interrupted with a vicious poke of the pistol barrel at the ample belly. The sheriff produced the key, grumbling as he shakily removed the cuffs.

Dancer rubbed his wrists, then thrust the manacles at the lawman.

"Put 'em on," he ordered, adding, "and no backtalk." He punctuated his request with another brusque jab of the pistol barrel.

Harley Brock looked into the intense brown eyes before him, deciding suddenly and wisely to do whatever this man asked. He felt as if he had parted the brush and looked into the predatory gaze of a cougar. A shuddering chill shook the big man's overstuffed frame as his mind's eye saw his own name engraved in granite. The sheriff, not a bright man, knew danger when he faced it. A man would be better served stepping on a rattler than stomping this man's toes.

"My guns?"

"In that gunny sack yonder." Brock pointed with a nod of his shaggy head to a burlap bag resting on the floor in the well of the scarred desk across the room.

"Your horses, tack and such is down at the livery."

Dancer marched his captive to the storeroom, chaining him to the shelves where he himself had been held the previous night. He picked a dusty rag off the shelf, told the sheriff to open up, then stuffed it in his mouth. He took the kerchief from around the sheriff's neck and tied it in place around the gag.

Emptying the cylinder of the lawman's pistol and pocketing the cartridges, Dancer tossed the gun into the big man's lap.

"Someone will most likely find you in a few hours, Harley. I didn't do that killing, and you'd be well advised not to pursue the matter. I got nothing particular against you, and I'd hate to kill you . . . but I'm a man does what's before me to do."

Dancer turned and walked through the door, closing it behind him. The sheriff heard the bar drop in place, then the click of the padlock. With a sigh, he wriggled around to make himself as comfortable as possible.

With rifle and shotgun over his left shoulder, one handgun in his holster, the other in back of his belt, Dancer proceeded down the middle of the street to the livery stable. The first gray of dawn was lightening the sky to the east where puffy little clouds floated like breakfast biscuits spilled from the pan.

A bewhiskered hostler was asleep on the straw in a stall near the door, snoring loudly. With each exhalation of fetid breath, the horse tender's flaccid lips fluttered to spew forth a fine whiskey mist. An uncorked, evidently depleted jug was cradled in the crook of the old man's right arm. Dancer stood over him, smelled his fiery breath, and knew there would be no necessity to bind him. The man had incapacitated himself quite efficiently.

Again in possession of all his outfit, Jack Dancer walked his horses the length of the street, leaving the shadowed bank of gray-board buildings in the direction he had come. He paused to unsaddle the dun and loose its picket, leaving it to graze on the lush grass at the side of the rutted road. Leather creaked as he turned in the saddle to look past the shabby street of the town to the sun peeking over the crest of the mountain.

"I'll be back, Raindance."

Chapter Five

With a gentle jab of booted heels, Dancer nosed the prancing appaloosa stallion further into the forest, climbing steadily toward the higher peaks and the solitude of the Sawatch Range of the Rockies. These peaks, vertebrae in the backbone of a continent, hold the hidden headwaters of the great rivers and, from haughty heights, direct their flows to vast oceans east or west.

The magnificent mountain country filled the lone horse-man with exultation and a joy of living. For the past few years, Jack Dancer had counted the sky and earth as his home, not logs or sawed timbers. Here, in this pristine wilderness, he was free of the crushing encroachment of tacky towns and settlements like Raindance, posing as civilization. Free from those swarming fortune seekers and land grabbers that stamped the label of "progress" on the spoilage of the land left in their wakes.

Sloe–eyed, black– and white–tailed deer curiously eyed the passage of man and mount through the towering avenues of Ponderosa pine and Douglas fir interspersed with aspen and spruce. A Rocky Mountain jay scolded the rider for his intrusion, but the hermit thrush and mountain chickadees, intent upon their constant chores of food-gathering, seemed to pay him no heed. The air was thin and brittle and clear. Dancer breathed deeply, seeking the perfume of the lovely anemone, ladies' slipper and columbine that brightened the clearings.

He pulled up at the point where a small stream met the lip of a great cliff, its crystal flow leaping into space with reckless abandon to join the tumbling river at the bottom of the canyon hundreds of feet below. The opposite wall of the canyon, seamed and weathered smooth by the ages, shone brilliantly in the afternoon sunlight of the red and yellow rock that gave the state its name, Colorado.

Jack dismounted, unsaddled the appaloosa and relieved the seventeen-hand blood bay of its packs. He turned the animals loose on the sweet grasses of the clearing, not bothering with tethers, as he knew they would not stray. He grinned as the frisky horses rolled on their backs, then romped like colts before settling down to graze.

Dancer put together a small cookfire and walked to fill his coffeepot with water from the icy spring. He dumped in a double handful of ground Arbuckle's coffee and set the pot in the fire. The water would take longer to boil at this altitude, a bit under eleven thousand feet, he reckoned, judging by the plant life around him. Across the canyon he could see three or four razor-edged summits he calculated would top fourteen thousand. There must be half a hundred that high in these Colorado Rockies. As he waited for the coffee to make, Dancer chewed some dried venison from his stores and watched the ascending white specks on the mountainside above the timberline across the way—a family of bighorn sheep.

Fugitive he may be, but at this moment, in this place, Jack Dancer was at peace. He would camp here a day or two, let things settle a bit, down in Raindance, then wander back there to see if he could put a few things right. Dancer was not a man to run from trouble, and would tolerate no mark against his name.

When Linda Macklin heard the news of a strange rider bringing in her father's horse, its saddle smeared with blood and Rad Macklin missing, she had acted quickly and decisively.

Linda dispatched the four hands that rode for the Flying M to the spot where the horse had reportedly been found, instructing them to split up and search out her father, not to return without him. Then she saddled her own mare and, with food for three days in her saddlebags, a bedroll and a slicker tied behind the cantle and a rifle in the saddle scabbard, rode at a gallop from the ranchyard, embarked upon her own search.

The distraught daughter rode the first day until it was too dark to continue, and slept the night in a cold camp in a grove of sheltering fir trees. Up and saddled at the first anemic hint of daylight to filter through the green canopy over her head, Linda had thrown together a quick breakfast of cold biscuits and coffee, then had resumed her all-consuming quest.

Now she stood on a rock shelf overlooking a small, secluded canyon, sighting down the blue-black barrel of her rifle at the stranger below. The unfamiliar rider stopped, hiked one lanky leg over the pommel of his saddle and looked leisurely about. From that distance his features were indistinct, but Linda saw that he was a tall, well-set-up man, broad through the shoulders and slim in the hips. His movements were fluid and graceful. She recognized the appaloosa he rode as an exceptionally fine animal, deep in the chest, built for speed and endurance. It was no cowpony, one could be sure. A flicker of fear rippled up her spine. Too often such a horse was ridden by a man expecting pursuit. Was this strange rider an outlaw then? Wary as she was, Linda could not help but appraise him with admiration. Outlaw perhaps, but this one was all the man a woman could want.

Cautiously, she drew back from the lip of the shelf toward the dark mouth of the cave behind her. The strange rider's eyes came up, leisurely scanning the area. Had he seen her? She hurried into the shelter of the cave, rifle at the ready.

Dancer had caught a slight flicker of movement from the tail of his eye. Something had moved on the rocky overlook, something not of the forest. Showing no reaction to the sighting, he moved on until well out of sight of any watcher from above. Finding a clearing with good grass and the trickling seep of a spring, Dancer unburdened his horses and picketed them on the lush forage, still damp with early dew in this shaded retreat. Intricate, beautiful, lacy-leafed ferns grew in deep profusion at the feet of the forest behemoths whose lofty crowns, on this morning, were hidden in the pewter-colored mists that crept into the clefts, crevices and groins of the mountains. The manhunter went to his packs and pulled out a pair of moccasins. He sat on a moss-covered log, removed his boots and put them on.

He got to his feet, carefully checked his rifle and sidearm and ghosted into the forest, back the way he had come and upslope.

Like a cat, Dancer moved unhurriedly and silently through the trees. He placed each moccasined foot down with care so that no twig would snap, no pebble would roll. He was a man who had spent much time in the forests and mountains of the West and his stealth and ability on the trail had become as natural to him as breathing. This was now his milieu. The man had evolved into a denizen of the wilds as much as the wolf, the deer, the grizzley.

Jack studied the shelf where he had seen the movement.

The rocky surface gave sparse evidence of what, or who, had been there, but smudges in the dust and several crushed needles told him that something had entered the dark recesses of the cave. His sixgun slipped easily to his hand.

"Don't move, mister. I've got a rifle trained on your belt buckle and, believe me, I won't miss. Put down your weapons."

It was the voice of a young woman. A woman who sounded as though she knew the practical application of the words she had spoken. Slowly, without any threatening gestures, Dancer laid his rifle and pistol on the rock surface in front of him.

With mincing steps, Linda Macklin emerged from the dark opening in the mountainside, her rifle's single black eye regarding the stranger in black. She squinted as the sun struck her squarely in the face.

With the quickness of a rattler's strike, Dancer's arm whipped forward. He grabbed the rifle barrel, twisting and plucking the gun from her grasp. Startled, the girl turned to dash back into the cave. Dancer grabbed her by the back of the belt and held her off the ground, legs churning and arms flailing.

"Whoa up there, little lady. I'm not going to hurt you. What in blazes you doing way up here by yourself, anyhow? Who are you?"

Upright again, Linda whipped around to face him, her manner angry and defiant, her blazing eyes as hostile as cornflower blue can get.

"You big bully! You've no right to manhandle me."

"Well now, sister. You had me under the gun. I reckon that's right enough to call for an answer or two."

Jack took a good look at her then. The young woman was seething with anger and frustration, but it could not mar her beauty. She stood haughty and proud, her golden hair capturing the sunlight. Small, perhaps 5'2", she must have weighed what it took to fill that space to perfection. Dressed in a man's shirt and tight denim pants, her supple figure spoke in eloquent denial of the masculinity of her wardrobe. She moved with the fluid grace of a muleskinner's whip. A slender waist over well-rounded hips led Dancer's eyes down her shapely legs to small, booted feet and slowly up again over the scenic route to her lovely face, a face that belonged in oils on canvas. A peaches and cream complexion, accented by a sprinkling of tiny freckles across her button of a nose, and full, sensuous lips slightly pouted, caused him to gasp in appreciation.

"Inspection over?" she asked in a low, throaty voice that stirred him.

"Yes'm. And well worth the price of the ticket." He opened his barn-door smile.

"Good. Perhaps now you'll go away and leave me alone. I've trouble enough without entertaining sightseers."

"Well, sister, happens yours isn't the only wildcat in the sack. I've come by a bit of a mess on my own boots . . .

"Seems one of your locals got himself bushwhacked. I found his horse wandering loose and led him into town. Now, I never laid eyes on this Rad Macklin hombre, but they unlimbered a new rope, figuring to hang me for killing him. So I just naturally took out of there. I need to find this man's body, then corral whoever shot him, to clear my name.

"But don't you be afraid, miss. I didn't kill this Macklin, or anybody else in these parts."

"No, you didn't, son."

Dancer whirled about at the resonance of the masculine reply to see a man standing in the mouth of the cave, leaning on a makeshift crutch. The new player's shirt hung open, revealing a bloody bandage on his side. The man looked about done in, his eyes dark hollows in a face the shade of cave mold. There was a gun in his hand.

The wounded man hobbled out and eased himself painfully onto a rock, keeping the barrel of his .45 trained on the manhunter.

"I'm Macklin."

A cup in her hand, Linda picked up a smoke-smudged enameled pot from the fire's edge, helped herself, then poured Jack's cup full of the steaming black liquid. After returning the pot to the fire, she crossed over to sit beside her father. She tested his brow with the back of her hand. He jerked his head to the side, not liking the fuss. He was looking as used-up as sheep pasture, and pale as a fresh-washed bed sheet.

Macklin was an ordinary-looking man of average height and weight. About fifty-five, Dancer guessed. His thick mop of hair, gray at the temples and sideburns, was snarled and tangled and soaked with sweat. Bushy brows hung like swallow's nests on the craggy cliff of his face. A full, graying mustache obscured his upper lip. His mouth was drawn as thin as the cutting edge of an ax. Deep furrows of fatigue had all but erased the etched lines of humor at the corners of his red and weepy eyes, sunken and dark-circled from the strain of his wound. He tended to jerk at the slightest sound from the forest, like a mistreated dog.

At the onset, Dancer and the Macklins had been wary of one another. But having discovered there was nothing to fear, they had fallen into serious conversation, discussing the bizarre circumstances that had thrown them together and seeking solutions to the problems at hand.

"Your daddy needs a doctor, ma'am. I'll watch him while you ride into town and fetch one here. If I show down there before things are cleared up, there's apt to be lead flying every which way."

"No."

"No?"

"You don't understand, Mr. Dancer. No one must know my father is alive. They will try again to kill him."

"You don't know that. The owlhoot that shot him was most likely just a road agent after his poke. Probably long gone by now.

"Aside from that, 'til he shows his face in town, I'm still wanted for *murder*."

"My daughter is right, Mr. Dancer. I'm terribly sorry you got dragged into this, and I couldn't fault you if you forced me into town with you to prove your innocence. But that was no robbery. Someone means to see me dead. There have been two previous attempts on my life. From ambush, just like this time."

"Who wants you dead? And why?"

"That's just it," Linda replied in her father's stead, "we don't have the foggiest notion. The Flying M is a small operation. There is plenty of other land around for the taking, so it surely isn't a land grab. And we are certainly not well off enough financially to precipitate any action like this."

Dancer turned to Macklin. "What about enemies? Have you stepped on any sore toes hard enough in the past to bring on a grudge killing?"

"What man doesn't have a few enemies? But no, nothing of that sort. I am afraid that I have led a rather drab and uneventful existence, Mr. Dancer . . . seldom making waves. I work hard, pull my own weight and I mind my own affairs. I know no man who'd wish to kill me."

"Then you have something that somebody wants . . . enough to kill for it. Think, man, think."

Linda looked at Jack with soulful eyes. The crystal tear that found its way slowly down her silken cheek gave testimony to the fear and frustration she was feeling.

"Please, Mr. Dancer . . . Jack. Won't you help us?"

Well, that did it. Following a man's trail, facing a renegade's gun or living off the wild country, Dancer was as good as the best. But against a beautiful woman's troubled tears he had amassed no defenses. How could a man resist a plea from so pretty a face? Dancer knew he was treed. Besides, as long as folks believed Macklin dead, he would be on the dodge. He had no recourse but to get to the bottom of it.

The Macklins needed food and medical supplies if they were to stay hidden in the mountains. Dancer left them what supplies he had from his own stores and started down the mountain for the Flying M.

The wary rider did not travel in a direct line to the ranch, but took a diversionary, roundabout route. It was a simple practice of habit developed over the years that had saved his scalp more than once. Approaching the ranch from the west, Dancer sat his mount a long while among the slender, straight trunks of a cloistered stand of aspen. Then, his sense of survival satisfied, he checked his weapons and made his way down the slope to the Macklin spread.

Linda had filled Jack in on the four riders that rode for the brand. Three were newly hired, temporary help for the spring branding and roundup. She assured him that the other man, their foreman, Quint Hawkes, was a good hand and could be trusted. Hawkes would stand.

Dancer rode into the ranchyard with his rifle across the bow of his saddle. A rangy, rawboned cowhand with sandy hair, rugged features, sloping shoulders and a mighty big shotgun nested in the crook of his arm stepped out to challenge him.

"Hold up, stranger. What's your business here?"

Dancer recognized the unmistakable sound of Fort Worth in the tall man's drawl-drenched query.

"I was told to ask for Quint Hawkes."

"I'm Hawkes. Who told you?" He was flint, looking for a stone to strike.

"Macklin sent me."

"Macklin?" The surprised cowboy's jaw dropped to his belt buckle. "He's alive?"

"Could hardly have sent me otherwise . . . but he's hurt. Been shot and needs your help. Now how about dropping the business end of that scatter gun? I'm a nervous man."

"How do I know you're tellin' the truth? I never seen you before."

"Reckon you don't, but I'm not about to sit here on my back pockets all day and jaw over it.

"His daughter Linda is with him. They're hid out. They need grub and medicine, and they need it now. Let me put it to you this way, partner . . . put the shotgun aside or start shooting."

Dancer eased his rifle in line with the top button of the cowhand's shirt.

Hawkes noticed the granite set of the stranger's jaw, the ease with which he handled the rifle, and the chill, unwavering gaze of the brown eyes that stared through him like the open barrels of matched sixguns.

"Light down and let's get 'er done," Hawkes said as he turned toward the wide, shaded porch of the ranchhouse.

Jack did not know yet if he could trust the Texan, but he saw no other recourse. So he told Hawkes how he had happened onto the Macklins, and of his run-in with the hemp-happy law of Raindance.

They loaded the supplies on two pack horses. Dancer turned to the foreman.

"I'll tell you how to get there. You take the goods on up. But be mighty careful, Hawkes. Nobody must know Macklin is alive. If anybody crosses your trail, you tell them that you're pulling your freight . . . your boss being dead and his daughter out of pocket, leaves no one to pay your wages. Hear?"

Hawkes nodded.

"Meanwhile," Dancer said, "I'm going to nose around and see if I can get a handle on what's going on here. Tell Macklin I'll be up in a couple of days."

The Flying M foreman left the ranchyard, pack horses in

tow, and disappeared into a sun-dappled aisle in the trees, following the stranger's directions toward the cave.

Dancer lingered a bit to get the lay of the ranch. The rambling one-story house looked to be no more than four or five years old. It was well constructed of carefully sized and fitted logs from the local forests. A large, native stone chimney stood at one end of the house, a smaller one at the opposite end. That would be the kitchen. Forty feet from the kitchen door stood a covered well, beside it a smokehouse. Twenty yards further along at the end of a well-worn path was a plank outhouse. Two-holer by the looks of it. Several hundred feet away stood a small bunkhouse of even more recent vintage, also of logs, its single window curtained with burlap. Behind the bunkhouse was another outhouse and two corrals, the smaller of the pens having a snubbing post and a gelding chute. A three-sided south-facing shed with eight stalls and a blacksmith's forge formed one side of the larger corral. Four good-looking horses—a black, a buckskin and two sorrels—stood hipshot in the smaller pen, arranged so that the swishing of their tails kept their neighbor's flanks free of the persistent flies that hovered like a gray cloud around them. A single spring-fed watering trough was situated to serve both enclosures. Nice little place, thought Dancer.

As he turned his horse to leave, Dancer thought he detected a shadow of movement at the burlap curtain in the bunkhouse window. He rode away, but under cover of the same thick stand of quaking aspen upslope of the ranch, he turned back to watch as three men stole cautiously from the bunkhouse door. He figured them to be the other Flying M hands, the temporary help, and he recognized their type at once as hardcases. Not typical ranchhands, they looked the part and fit the call of men who sell their guns to the highest bidder. Had Macklin hired them for their fighting skills, or was he ignorant of their nature? It was something to think on.

Chapter Six

They were a scurvy crew, ruthless and amoral.

Virgil Patch and Manfred Worthy had been together since the war, had ridden with the raiders of Bloody Bill Anderson. Gunwise and without principles or scruples to hinder them. They were big men, in weathered hats with the brims curled down in front and dirty dusters over their clothes, the tails split for riding.

Patch was the larger of the two, topping six feet and lean, with a blue chin and thick black mustache languishing under a pushed-in nose that had long ago been broken in several places, causing his breath to come in short wheezes and whistles. Tiny eyes and a razor-slash of a mouth seemed crowded out of their rightful positions in his face by the trouble-broadened proboscis. Probably a handsome face, the observer allowed, if you were a bitch wolf.

Worthy was thick-set, weighing as much as his companion but several inches shorter. His belly hung out over his belt like bread dough on the rise. His large head, swarthy complexion and full black beard gave him the look of a bear in man's clothing. He gripped the short, cold stub of a cigar in yellowed teeth. The gold-rimmed spectacles perched on the spacious bridge of a vulture's beak of a nose had thick lenses, giving his magnified eyes the appearance of a predatory owl on the hunt.

Both Patch and Worthy were dangerous men. Not so fierce or vicious or lethal, though, as the third man, the half-breed Comanche called Stone Wolf. Even his companions feared him and no one knew how many men, women and children Stone Wolf had slaughtered for their meager possessions, or merely because their presence had irritated him. The man was a mixed-blood predator possessing the ambiguity of two cultures and the discipline of neither. A chill of premonition crept up the spine of Jack Dancer as he observed the Indian from his vantage point in the aspen grove. He was filled with the certainty that one day soon he would face this man over a gun barrel or the point of a knife. The evil in the man was a tangible thing.

The three men stood peering into the forest after Hawkes and Dancer.

"Now what in tarnation you suppose that was about?"

"I ain't sure. Them pack horses was loaded heavy. You don't reckon Macklin's still alive and holed up somewheres, do you?"

"Alive, my hindmost! I tell you I got him clean. Took him right out of the saddle."

"Yeah, Patch, but you never checked the body, you said. Maybe . . ."

"I told you, dadgum it, somebody was coming. I had to hightail it." Patch was puffed up like a bloated steer on bad feed, resenting the slight on his ability as a bushwhacker.

"Who was that other bad-lookin' hombre?"

"Never seen him before, but this here's something we'd best tell the boss."

"Ha! You tell him, then. If Macklin is alive, he'll be fit to be tied. He's apt to have our hides. I'm for followin' Quint. See where he's off to with all them goodies."

"Yeah. Let's saddle up."

Dancer was dead-and-buried tired, his body demanding repayment of the sleep he had missed. The events of the past few days had left him feeling emotionally flogged.

Stopping often to check his backtrail, he kept a practiced eye peeled for a place to bed down for the night. He sought a spot that offered shelter, but that also was defensible. He knew from long, hard experience the consequences exacted upon the incautious in the wild. Topping a rise he came suddenly upon a long-deserted trapper's cabin; shabby, ramshackle, box-like, innocent of amenities. But in his exhausted state it rivaled the happy hearth of home.

Keeping to the cover of the trees, Dancer rode carefully around the shack before approaching. Then, seeing nothing to alarm his senses, he entered the overgrown clearing. A small pole corral and a deteriorating shed stood behind the cabin. He unsaddled the appaloosa and turned it into the corral. Taking a Green River knife from the sheath at his belt, he cut an armload of grass from in front of the shed and dumped it onto the hoof-cratered floor of the pen for the horse.

Rifle in hand, he pushed open the plank door of the cabin, struck a match and entered the dark interior, clearing cobwebs as he advanced. There had been no man here for years. He found a rodent-nibbled stub of a candle on the dirt floor beside a fallen table. He lit the blackened wick with the shortening match in his fingers and placed the candle on a stone shelf above the crumbling fireplace. The weary traveler took a careful survey of the room. A bunk against the far wall, not to be out-dilapidated by the table, had collapsed. The floor was packed earth. One shuttered window faced south onto the slope. The geriatric structure was a one-room affair, maybe twelve by fifteen feet. Snug and tight.

The last wayfarer, long ago, had been thoughtful enough to leave a supply of firewood. Dancer would return the favor before he left. Using a packrat's nest for tinder, he built a hat-sized fire and returned to the corral for his gear. With water from his canteen he started a pot of coffee and spread his bedroll on the hard-packed earth before the frolicking flames of the fire. Using his saddle for a pillow, he lay down to wait for the coffee to make. He never heard the pot pop as the last of the coffee boiled away.

Quint Hawkes' neck swiveled constantly, his eyes darting from tree to tree. He twisted often in the saddle to search the dark trail behind him. The Flying M foreman was growing increasingly nervous and watchful as he neared the spot where he hoped to find Macklin and the girl. They had been good friends to a lonesome cowpoke and he wanted to be darn sure he was bringing them help and not trouble.

Hawkes had been a down-at-the-heels, out-of-work Texas wrangler, flat broke and hungry, when he first met Rad Macklin. Stranded in a strange country with nothing but a worn saddle and the trail-tattered clothes on his back. Having overheard Hawkes' plea for work at the livery in Abilene, Macklin had invited the gaunted trailhand to have dinner with him, his first meal in three days. The rancher had watched with a gratified smile as Quint wolfed down his vittles. The two men had taken to each other right off, and Macklin, recognizing Hawkes' knowledge of ranching and cattle, had hired him to help run his new spread in the Colorado Rockies. Quint had been here as ramrod with the Flying M ever since.

And, of course, there was Linda. Quint Hawkes had been in love with her from the moment he had set eyes on her, though the big, lonely cowhand was the only one who knew. Most likely the only one who would ever know.

Hawkes saw no indication of anyone on his backtrail, but he had a nagging feeling that someone was following. Someone who did not want to be seen. Giving credence to his suspicions, he decided to pull up and take a closer look. Tying the horses to low-hanging branches at the side of the faint trail he followed, the lanky foreman sneaked back through the woods to watch.

Quint squatted in dense cover for half an hour, occasionally switching positions when his legs cramped, checking and rechecking the rifle in his hands, wiping his sweaty palms on his pant legs. Hawkes had spent his life on a cowpony. On the move. He had no taste for waiting or hiding in the woods. His concentration wavered and he decided he must be jumping at shadows. He rose to leave.

Then he heard them. Horses coming up the trail. Hawkes cocked his rifle, training the sight where the horsemen must appear. He recognized Patch and Worthy as they came into view, their eyes lowered to concentrate on the trail before them. He stepped from hiding.

"Hold up, boys. Just where you figger you're going?"

Startled, the pair drew rein. Patch grinned widely without a trace of humor.

"Hawkes. Pardner, are we glad to see you. Thought there for a while we'd lost you."

"I ain't yours to find or lose. What you doin' here? You'd ought to be at the ranch earnin' your wages."

"Well, now, that there's no way to talk. We seen you head out from the ranch with them pack animals. We just figured you might of stumbled into trouble . . . and bein' saddlemates, we naturally come to see could we help."

"No trouble. Don't need help. You two hightail it back to the spread. I'll be along directly."

Patch's eyes darted to something behind the foreman.

Hawkes turned, too slow. Stone Wolf's knife plunged to the hilt just under the rib cage. Hawkes' eyes bulged wide, his heavy jaw dropped open in a silent scream that buried itself as a hoarse, sawing rattle deep in his lungs. He clutched at the wound, falling against his attacker. The sneering Comanche pushed at him, freeing the bloodied blade with a moist, sucking sound as Hawkes fell away. Patch and Worthy came rushing forward.

"You ignorant heathen," Worthy shouted, "now he can't tell us where he was headed! Blast your worthless hide!"

The gunman's anger died a sudden death when he saw the fierce fury building in the Indian's eyes. He realized he had made a serious blunder. Stone Wolf would kill him as willingly as he had killed Hawkes, no matter that they were supposed to be allies, part of the same outfit. Shivering like a dog passing bones, Worthy quickly assumed an apologetic look.

"Aw, I'm sorry, Stone Wolf. Weren't your fault, he give you no choice. Why, he had me and Patch here under the gun. You might of saved our skins. No hard feelin's?"

Glaring at Worthy, Stone Wolf walked over and grabbed him by the beard, pulling the bulky badman almost out of the saddle. He placed the knife at the quaking outlaw's throat, wiped the blade free of blood on his neckerchief, then turned and disappeared into the trees as silently as he had come, not saying a word.

Patch and Worthy looked at each other.

"That there's one scary sonofagun!"

Dancer spent the day riding on and around the Flying M range searching for some clue as to why Rad Macklin was marked for murder.

It was good cattle country with plenty of graze and good water, but it was no better than a lot of the surrounding range and the ranch was not large by western standards—a couple of thousand acres at most. Nor did he see any likely ground for mining. There was good timber, but no roads, and again, there was good timber growing all over the neighboring mountains.

There had to be a reason for death to be stalking the rancher, but it apparently was not the ranch itself. So Dancer figured it had to be something on the ranch, something hidden from view—or something personal regarding Macklin himself, or his daughter, Linda. A reason that they were hiding, were not considering, had overlooked or forgotten.

Well, he would camp here tonight, then ride over tomorrow to talk to the Macklins. Maybe he could stir their memories, pick their brains to come up with some intimation, hint or clue that would give him a tack to take toward solving this puzzle. He was sure enough shooting blanks at shadows so far.

After he had banked his fire and settled in his blankets for the night, Dancer lay awake, arms folded beneath his head, gazing up through a black web of branches at the night sky. A little pale moon hung in a corner of the sky, faint as a dusty thumb print on a window pane. The pulsating chorus of ground frogs joined in concert with the amorous arias of crickets. An owl glided noiselessly across the moon. A coyote, on a ridge miles away, split the night with a piercing lament of loneliness.

His mind's eye brought the remembered vision of Linda Macklin into view. *That is one fine-looking woman.* Jack's thoughts were less than pure as he drifted off to sleep.

Linda was practically bouncing off the musty walls of the cave, fraught with worry. Neither Dancer nor Hawkes had shown up with the desperately needed supplies. Her father must have medical attention. He had been running a high fever, and several times he became delirious, rambling and ranting in disconnected remembrances of his past. He kept calling for his wife, Rebecca, Linda's mother, now long dead and buried. And he had begun to cough, deep racking upheavals, undoubtedly an effect of the dampness of the cavern's interior.

The meager supply of food that Dancer had left for them was depleted. She could not even put together a hot broth for her ailing father. Nor did she dare go afield to hunt for meat, for fear that someone would hear the shot and discover that Rad Macklin was not dead. She paced the gloomy cave, then walked outside to the edge of the shelf, searching the surrounding trees, wringing her hands in concern and desperation.

As he neared the place of hiding, Dancer spied Linda standing in profile at the cliff's edge, the softly rounded contours of her striking silhouette competing with the view. Linda's contours won. He rode forward, calling out as he neared so as not to startle her.

Jack dismounted and tied the appaloosa to a dead snag, sprang to the rock shelf and crossed toward the fretting female. She whirled to face him.

"Where in *blazes* have you been?"

Before he could reply, Linda jumped toward him, threw her arms around his neck and kissed him fervently, passionately. Then, as quickly, she drew back facing him, her body aquiver, tears rolling down her cheeks.

In a broken voice, almost a whisper, she said, "I . . . I'm sorry. I don't know what came over me. It's only that I've been so frightened. Daddy . . . he's very sick. Forgive me please, Mr. Dancer."

"No need, ma'am. My pleasure," Dancer replied. Then he smilingly added, "but maybe in light of our new relationship you'd best call me Jack."

Linda smiled coyly, blushing, then asked, "Did you bring the supplies?"

"You mean Hawkes isn't here? I sent him on ahead immediately. He had everything. Should have been here day before yesterday."

"Oh, my Lord. No, we haven't seen him. Something must have happened to him too." Her face darkened once again with gloom and worry.

"Could be he just took off, wanting no part of this trouble."

"No! No, Quint would never do that. He is more than a good hired hand, Jack, he is a family friend. Honest, dependable and afraid of nothing that I've seen. No, he is in trouble somewhere. I know it."

They went into the cavity in the bluff. Dancer knelt beside the wounded man and pressed his hand to the glistening forehead. It was hot, real hot. Macklin opened his rheumy eyes and tried to speak, breaking instead into a coughing spasm. Jack looked up into the concerned face of Linda Macklin.

"Linda, we've got to move him. He'll die here for sure."

"But where? There's nowhere."

"Back to the ranch. To his own bed. I'll sneak into Raindance and get some medicine, and he needs some hot food in him. It's his only chance."

"What if they come to kill him?"

"Everyone believes he's dead already. All we have to do now is *bury him*!"

Chapter Seven

The wick of the last lit lantern had ceased smoking when Dancer stole like a shadowy specter into the black, quiet streets of Raindance, come for the badly needed medical supplies. He filled his mental list from the shelves of the emporium by the faint, flickering light of a match cupped in his palm, left a double eagle on the counter to pay for what he had taken, and returned unnoticed to the ranch. Leaving Linda to tend her father's worsening condition, he issued terse instructions that she admit no one to the ranchhouse during his absence, even a close friend. Then, when the eastern sky began to lighten, Dancer set out to discover what had happened to Quint Hawkes and the pack horses.

The Flying M foreman was still lying where he had fallen in a dark pool of congealed blood when Dancer came upon the fly-swarmed body. As the early sun chased the lingering gloom from beneath the lush boughs of the pines, he methodically screened the ground at the scene, finding the hoofprints of two mounted horses, prints he would know if he saw them again. He also found the mark of a moccasin near the body. Dancer catalogued these observations in his memory, to be recalled and used as needed.

Taking a blanket from the bedroll behind his saddle, Jack prepared to wrap Hawkes' body for transport back to the ranch. When he turned the cowboy over he heard a faint groan!

Dancer could scarce believe that the spark of life still glimmered in the foreman's limp, gray carcass, so brutally violated. He bent his ear to Hawkes' gaping mouth and detected a slight stirring of breath. The man was alive. Barely, hanging on by a short whisker, but alive. Hurriedly then, he draped Hawkes over the saddle of the sidestepping, blood-shy appaloosa, tying his hands and feet under the belly of the horse with rawhide thongs. Leading the horse afoot he started briskly back to the Flying M. He had not gone far when he heard a horse's plaintive whickering from the brush. Hawkes' sorrel came trotting through the trees, delighted for the company. Jack mounted the sorrel and headed for the barn, bloody cargo in tow.

The bare wood coffin, filled with enough dirt, debris and rocks to approximate the weight of Rad Macklin, had been nailed tightly shut and was beside the freshly dug grave on a knoll near the Flying M ranchhouse. A carved stone, complete with name, dates and proper sentiment stood somberly at the head of the six-foot opening in the earth.

Linda Macklin, draped forlornly in black, dabbed at her eyes with a dainty hanky that had been steeped in horse liniment to assure secretion of ample tears for her obligatory mourning. A few neighbors stood in reverent attendance and the preacher was there, Good Book in hand. Patch, Worthy and Stone Wolf had not reappeared at the ranch after the attack on Hawkes, so Linda had gone into town to hire a pair of idlers to dig and fill in the grave.

A brilliant flash of lightning bulged a cloud with livid flames as the coffin was ceremoniously lowered into the yawning excavation on the hill. The preacher prayed long and fervently, the ladies wept, and the hole was filled. Linda stepped forward, solemnly placing a bouquet of fresh wild-flowers on the mounded grave. Had the mourners been looking in the direction of the ranchhouse they might have detected a shadow behind the curtain of a bedroom window.

"Kind of chilling for a man to witness his own funeral." Macklin made his observation as a slight smile teased the corners of his mouth. "You think we fooled those who wanted me dead?"

Dancer shrugged. "No tellin'. We'll know soon enough I expect. Now you crawl back under those covers or Linda will have your scalp and mine too."

Macklin was looking and feeling much better after four days of proper care and rest, though still far from recuperated. His cough had vanished and there was now some color to him.

Critically wounded, Quint Hawkes lay in a bed in the same room. The foreman had gained consciousness on several occasions and had taken some nourishment, but he was too weak and too sick to disclose what had befallen him. Dancer had a fair notion, anyhow. The three men he had evaluated at the bunkhouse that day had not been seen since. Their horses were gone from the corral, their clothes from the bunkhouse. He had seen a moccasin print where he found Hawkes. One of those men, the coffee-skinned one, had worn moccasins. Could be they were the ones who wanted Macklin dead, or more likely, worked for someone who did.

Dancer and her father remained muted and hidden from view while Linda had the mourners in for tea, coffee and cakes in the sitting room. After the last tearful departure, she came into the bedroom.

"Hi, Daddy. How are you feeling?"

Rad motioned with a broad thumb over his shoulder to the fresh grave on the knoll.

"Sure enough beats the alternative," he said.

* * *

Court Blaine stood in his room above the Golconda Saloon in Raindance, staring through the droplet-splattered window at the quagmire the rain was making of the street below. The smoke from the long cigar he was turning slowly in his fingers hung in a layer of blue haze just above his head.

He was a big man, two inches over six feet, barrel-chested, slender at the waist. His dark hair was graying attractively at the temples and he sported a luxuriant mustache, waxed and twisted at the corners of his mouth. Blaine was dressed in a black broadcloth suit and wore a brocaded silk vest over his white ruffled shirt. A stick pin fashioned from a gold nugget accented his gray cravat. He sported a fetching smile on meatless lips when it suited his purpose, but the penetrating, cold green eyes that bored out from beneath his furrowed brow were humorless and cruel.

Blaine had listened to the report of the funeral services held at the Macklin ranch in silent satisfaction. The old man's daughter, he was told, had found the body and had taken it home, then come to town to order the stone and to have a coffin constructed. A little judicious prying had led the girl to reveal that Macklin had apparently crawled some distance after being shot and had hidden himself in thick brush, then succumbed to his wound, dead when she found him. In the telling, Linda had broken into tears and Blaine had comforted her, then had led her to the doctor's office for something to calm her grief. He wanted very much for Linda Macklin to consider him a friend.

Court Blaine had been born with another name in a tall two-and-a-half-story house that stood on a small, rocky farm of a few unproductive acres near a backwater community in the foothills of the Missouri Ozarks. His father had been a sharecropper and a drunkard, always dreaming of successes that were never to come. His mother was a sickly and whiny woman who constantly bemoaned her station in life.

Court had been a humorless child, did well in school, but had no friends and wanted none. Large for his age, the boy became a bully, terrorizing his classmates into catering to his whims and wants and needs.

By the time he was thirteen, even young Court's father was afraid of the intense, domineering youngster. The boy refused to help with the farm work and got a job at a general merchandise store in town. Court was a diligent worker who soon earned the confidence of his employer. The merchant's misplaced trust offered the scheming youth an opportunity to skim money from the store's receipts, by clever manipulation of inventory and accounts, recording sales for less than charged, or by overcharging aging, less attentive customers.

At fifteen, Court Blaine decided to strike out on his own. He burglarized his employer's store and two other establishments, then, lying about his age, enlisted in the Confederate Army. Blaine deserted his beleaguered unit when it became apparent that the tide of war, then in its fiercest hour, had changed. He connected with a gang of deserters, ruffians, misfits and outlaws commanded by one Jubal Blackthorn. Riding hard on sound horses, guns blazing indiscriminately, the renegades terrorized the frontier territories, operating in remote areas where the only law was measured in calibers. The marauders swooped across the unguarded land, preying on the unwary, the defenseless and the innocent, on isolated homesteads and small companies of travelers, on any victim helpless and hapless—like sharks in a feeding frenzy.

Blaine's size and toughness, and his total disregard for human life and the rights and property of others, soon led to his promotion within the ranks of the raiding rabble. He became second in command, lieutenant to Blackthorn him-

self, and as such garnered a larger share of the booty realized from the gang's pillage.

The prize of a lifetime presented itself to the outlaws when
they learned of a convoy of ore wagons from the newly discovered Climax diggings in what was then Colorado Territory.
The wagons were transporting high-grade ore across the
mountains to be milled in Denver. Finagling several members
of the raider band into positions as guards for the wagon train,
Blackthorn's marauders laid a successful ambush, swooping
to kill a dozen armed outriders and escape with the gold, leaving no one alive to identify them as the culprits.

To avoid pursuit and discovery, Blackthorn decided to
transport the stolen ore to mills further south in the
Territory. They would all be rich men!

Well along the way, filled with the heady success of one
of the biggest highway robberies of all time, the gang paused
to celebrate. Encamped in a canyon, the ruthless men sat and
laughed around their fires, drinking heavily and dreaming of
the pleasures that their newly acquired riches would bring
them. Drunk with success and spirits, their caution dulled by
the celebration, they stood no chance when the Indians
attacked.

A party of young Ute braves, after horses, whiskey and
guns, descended upon the camp—whooping, slashing,
shooting, killing. Only two of the outlaw party escaped the
massacre—Jubal Blackthorn and Court Blaine.

The Indians departed with all they could carry, driving the
captured horses and mules before them. Cautious and shak-
en, the two survivors crept from hiding back to the scene of
the slaughter. The Utes had not been interested in the ore,
seeing no value to it. It remained in the wagons undisturbed.
But the Utes had driven off all the stock, so there remained
no way to move the plundered treasure.

Cursing, Blackthorn turned to his lieutenant.

"We got a long walk ahead of us, Court, but we ain't

licked. We'll steal some stock, pick up some men and come back for the gold. Then we'd best hide or bury it 'til things blow over. Let's go."

As Blackthorn pivoted to lead the way, Court Blaine lunged to plunge a knife into his leader's broad and unguarded back. Blackthorn turned, the knife protruding from the base of his neck, an incredulous expression on his twisted face.

"N–nothing can turn on a man more viciously than his own watchdog," the mortally wounded bandit muttered.

Blaine then put a bullet between his eyes.

He walked out of the wilderness, acquired a team of six mules to pull the wagons and returned alone to haul the stolen gold out of the canyon. It loomed as a monumental task for one man, but he felt that he could trust no hireling to help and to keep his secret. Unaccustomed to driving a six-mule rig, he was often frustrated, but after a period of trial-and-error practice and utilizing a researched string of muleskinner profanity, he managed. The treacherous lieutenant of the late Jubal Blackthorn made four trips to the death-drenched scene, one for each wagon. Under cover of darkness he transported the gold to a secluded valley in the Sawatch Range near the tiny town of Raindance.

Blaine dumped the rich ore from each wagon into an old buffalo wallow that had been enlarged and deepened by time, wind and runoff. Then he covered the covert treasure with dirt. He would then return to the scene of the massacre, leave an empty wagon, hitch his mules to one loaded with ore and repeat the process. Having completed the transfer of the stolen gold, Blaine burned and buried the last wagon, sold the mules and settled in the town of Raindance to await an opportune time to "discover" the treasure cache.

He bought into a saloon in Raindance with the hoarded spoils from his raiding career, renaming the establishment, with tongue in cheek, the Golconda, meaning "great wealth." Then the dapper renegade settled into the guise of a gambler, an avocation at which he had become quite skilled around the fires in outlaw and Army camps.

Blaine's only mistake was that he neglected to file claim to the valley where he had buried the gold. He had not thought it prudent at the time to call attention to the area, and so had waited—too long.

Rad Macklin had come to Raindance with a deed to the valley to establish a ranch there, building a house directly over the buffalo wallow where the gold was buried. Court Blaine had tried repeatedly to purchase the property, with no success. Macklin was not interested in turning a profit. The rancher explained that he wanted only to make a home for his daughter and to secure a haven in which to grow old.

That had been eight years ago. Blaine's frustration had grown with each day, escalating into a burning hatred of Rad Macklin. So he had recruited Patch, Worthy and Stone Wolf. He would have Macklin eliminated. No woman could run a ranch alone, or would want to, and he could surely arrange to buy the Flying M from Linda Macklin—and thus reclaim his fortune.

Now Macklin was dead and buried. Blaine planned to wait a respectable length of time for her grief to pale, then he would buy the ranch from Linda. He would sell off the gold in lots, as if mining it, then would leave this dreary, backward little part of the world and settle in New Orleans, where his wealth would make him an important and powerful man, and where money could buy any worldly pleasures. Palatial estates, fine clothes, fine wines. People would obey him, step aside for him. He would at last enjoy the station in life to which a man of his talents and abilities was suited and entitled.

"Dadgum it."

Dancer felt the bitter bite of frustration as he wheeled his

appaloosa in the direction of the Flying M ranchhouse and
nudged the big stallion into a lope with a jab of his heels. He
had never been so buffaloed, so completely at a loss to get
to the seat of a problem. He was seeking to discover who
had tried to murder Macklin and, equally as important, why
the rancher was marked for death. Macklin himself seemed
to have no clue. Dancer had been over every inch of the
Flying M with an experienced eye, searching for—what? A
hint. A direction. Some evidence of a motive for the
ambushes. All he had earned for his hours polishing a saddle was a chapped backside and a sour attitude.

Nor did it salve his sore temper that Dancer could not cir-
culate among folks who might recognize him as the escaped
"killer" of Rad Macklin, a restriction that further hampered
his investigation. In his profession as a hunter of men,
Dancer was a master at gleaning intelligence from bits and
pieces of information picked up in casual conversation in
saloons, dining halls, hotel lobbies and on the streets. That
ability had now been neutralized by his need to stay out of
the mean and squinty eye of the public.

Jack had only been passing through, headed for his home
range at the Gunnison. Now his whole life was stalled here,
in this secluded valley, until he could unravel the mystery
and prove himself innocent of murdering a man that was
currently bouncing off the walls of the Flying M ranchhouse.

There was a bright aspect to the quandary, though. Dancer
and Linda Macklin had become quite friendly, taking long
walks together, riding through the meadows and the mountains in shared appreciation of the beauty around them, talking for hours about their hopes and plans and dreams.

Linda was a strikingly handsome, intelligent woman with
a lively sense of humor and a laugh like wind chimes in the
mountain breeze. She enjoyed many of the same things in
which Jack, himself, took pleasure. He'd had no interest in
female company since his wife, Laura, had died. Linda

could be *the* woman. One to marry, to build a life around. *If* he, Jack Dancer, was ready to settle down, to relinquish the restless obsession that gripped him. A big if. Jack just did not know if he was ready.

But that was a decision he need not face right now. The immediate situation took precedence. Dancer would never be free to pursue a future of any kind until this matter could be resolved. Besides, he could not be certain that Linda felt that same way about him. She had not said as much since the kiss at the cave. He determined to put his relationship with Linda Macklin in the holding pen for the time being. First things first.

Rad Macklin was no longer confined to his sick bed. Able to use a cane, he was now skittering around the house like a three-legged doodlebug on hot sand. At Jack's urgings he confined himself to the indoors to avoid being seen by some chance passerby. Being restless, Macklin had taken over the care of his friend and foreman, Quint Hawkes, partly to have something to do and partly because he held himself responsible for what had befallen the lanky cowhand.

Hawkes was not healing as rapidly as had Macklin, for his wound had been more serious than the one his boss had received, and too, he had lain long on the forest floor. If Dancer had come upon him only an hour or two later, Quint's headstone would now stand on the knoll alongside Macklin's, with one big difference—that grave would contain a lanky Texas corpse.

The straw-haired cowboy was improved to the point that he could sit up in bed, feed himself and talk a little. He confirmed Dancer's suspicion that it had been the butchering Stone Wolf who had attacked him, and that Worthy and Patch had been accessories to the attempt on his life.

Were the three hardcases still around? In his wanderings,

Dancer had seen no sign of anyone near the ranch, but they could be in town or holed up somewhere else. It would depend, he supposed, upon what they were after and how deeply they were involved in the Macklin "killing."

Chapter Eight

A whicker from the appaloosa in the corral alerted Dancer to the presence of a rider coming up the rutted road from the direction of Raindance. Squinting his eyes he was able to identify a single horseman approaching at a canter ahead of a column of dust. Jack slipped quickly through the back door of the ranchhouse into the kitchen. Rad Macklin was sitting at the kitchen table having tea with his daughter.

"Rider coming, Macklin," Dancer said, grabbing the rancher's arm. "We'd best get out of sight."

Both men hustled off to the room where Hawkes still lay bedfast, leaving Linda to deal with the unidentified visitor.

The high-stepping black, lathered and blowing, had a white-blazed head that resembled a skull from a distance. The rider sat ramrod straight and proud in the saddle.

Court Blaine wore a tailored, dove-gray broadcloth coat that hung to mid–calf over black, pinstriped trousers. His white shirt was silk, elegantly ruffled. His tie, black. The flat–crowned hat he wore was of the style favored by gamblers on the riverboats of New Orleans and the Natchez Trace. The polished boots with walking heels were of soft black leather. He held a nosegay of gaily colored, fresh-cut flowers in his free hand.

"Who's the peacock?" Dancer wondered aloud, peeking through the sheer curtains at the bedroom window.

"Let me see." Macklin shouldered the taller man aside to peer at the visitor.

"Huh. It's Court Blaine, our resident card slick and all-purpose dandy. What y'suppose he wants?"

"Court Blaine?" Quint Hawkes lurched bolt upright, wincing at the pain of his sudden movement. "That glad-handin', bottom-dealin', sidewindin' son of . . ."

Macklin and Dancer whirled in unison toward the bedridden cowboy, their fingers to pursed lips.

"Sh-h-h!"

Blaine trotted his horse into the ranchyard, stopping at the hitch rail in front of the long, covered veranda. He dismounted nimbly, wrapped reins over the polished rail and looked around carefully, studying the yard and adjoining structures. His head stopped in mid-swivel as he spied the spotted stallion in the corral. He frowned, then shrugged. Taking the silk handkerchief from his breast pocket, Blaine slapped at his sleeves and shoulders, then stepped onto the porch and to the door.

At the gambler's rap, Linda walked to the door, pausing to smooth her apron and to tuck a stray wisp of hair into the bun at the back of her head. Clearing her throat and moistening her lips, she swung open the door.

"Miss Macklin."

Blaine removed his hat, holding it at his waist, and extended the bouquet of flowers, flashing a brilliant smile.

"Why, Mr. Blaine," Linda said in mock surprise. She accepted the flowers, raising them to her nose.

"Thank you. What brings you so far from town?"

"I've been concerned, Linda . . . may I call you Linda?"

She nodded.

"I've been concerned about your being way out here all by yourself. This is certainly not a country for a woman alone."

"But I am not alone, Mr. Blaine. I have a foreman."

"What? I thought . . ."

He caught himself. Court Blaine and his henchmen were the only ones who knew that Quint Hawkes' bones lay deep in the forest, picked clean now by magpies and coyotes.

"Thought what, Mr. Blaine?"

"I thought your foreman and your other hands had deserted you after your father was killed."

"Uh, yes, of course," Linda stammered. "I hired a new man, passing through on his way to Texas," she lied. "His name is . . . Smith. Boone Smith."

"Yes. Well, good. I hope he's a good man. Is that his horse in the corral? The appaloosa?"

She nodded.

"Fine animal. Anyway," he said, stalling, hoping to be invited inside, "I stand ready and eager to be of assistance in any way I can, Linda. I hope you will take me to heart on that offer."

Linda stood firm in the doorway, but smiled and thanked him for his thoughtfulness.

"By the way, there is a dance in town this Saturday. An annual affair, as you know, I'm sure. If you are feeling up to it, I would be honored if you would be my guest for dinner, then allow me to accompany you to the festivities." Blaine bowed low, smiling his most fetching smile.

"Well, I don't think . . . Yes. I will. I'd like that very much."

"Excellent. I'll call for you in my carriage Saturday evening at five. Good day, Linda."

The gambler bowed again, put on his hat, mounted the black mare and cantered from the yard, still smiling.

* * *

"What in tarnation's got into you, Miss Linda? That tinhorn's not the sort you'd ought to be keepin' company with. He's a gambler . . . a crooked one at that. Why, he's been after your daddy to sell him this place ever since we come here. That's the reason he's cozyin' up to you."

Hawkes laid back, exhausted by the effort of his outburst. Linda's face colored, her blue eyes sparking fire.

"Oh, is that so, Quint Hawkes? You think the only reason a man might possibly wish to spend time with me is to get my poor dead father's estate, is that it?

"Well let me tell you this, though it is certainly none of your business. I am a grown woman, and perfectly capable of conducting my own affairs, choosing my own friends and making my own decisions. Besides, Court Blaine is a very attractive man, and a gentleman with beautiful manners. Something we could use more of around here."

She wheeled on her heels and stomped fuming from the room.

"Wait, I didn't mean . . ."

Too late. Linda was out of earshot, already slamming pans around in the kitchen.

"Dagnab it, boss, you know I didn't mean no such thing."

Macklin grinned and shrugged. Hawkes turned to Dancer.

"Dancer, pardner, she likes you, and you got a way with words. Tell her, will you? Smooth it over for me?"

"Sorry, cowboy," Dancer said, chuckling. "You saddled that bronc, you ride it."

Hawkes fell back heavily on the bed with a sigh, an anguished expression on his face, as they closed the door behind them.

Dancer walked into the kitchen, watching with a half-smile as Linda blustered about, mumbling to herself. He pulled his hands from the back pockets of his jeans, stealing a cookie from a batch cooling on the counter.

"Boone Smith?" he asked.

As she turned to look at him, a mischievous smile began to form at the corners of her mouth.

"You like it?"

"Well, the 'Smith' is a mite plain for my tastes, but I kind of favor the 'Boone' part. You must figure I'm uncommonly crafty in the woods, huh?"

Linda smiled, a smile Dancer felt clear down to the soles of his boots. Then she said, "No, I once had a scruffy mongrel of a dog that I called Boone."

The rancher and the man accused of his murder squatted together on the kitchen stoop, relaxing after the evening meal. An eagle soared high over the meadow in the waning daylight, no doubt hoping for a bedtime snack. The nearby hills were lit by the fires of a setting sun. Somewhere in the pines a whippoorwill called.

Dancer turned to Macklin. "Hawkes allows as how this Blaine is mighty determined to have your ranch, Rad. Do you suppose he might be the one that wants you out of the way?"

A cloud of concentration drifted across Macklin's features, then he replied, "Hmm. No, I don't believe so. He offered to buy me out, true. Quite persistent about it, in fact. But he has never made any threats, nor even been unfriendly or hostile in our dealings together. No, my friend, I think we'd best look elsewhere."

At that moment, Stone Wolf was sitting on the edge of the maple desk in Blaine's quarters above the Golconda, absently fingering the keen point of the gleaming blade in his hand.

"Something strange is going on at that ranch," Blaine was saying. "I didn't see the new hand, but that spotted stallion looks like the one Sheriff Brock described as the horse that escaped prisoner was riding when they got him for killing

Macklin. That makes no sense, though. A man escapes the rope, he'd damn well leave the country, not go to work for the heirs of the man he's supposed to have killed. But it is odd that the girl didn't invite me inside.

"I want you to take a ride out there and look things over. Wait until Saturday. Miss Macklin will be with me, here in town. See that this new Flying M foreman understands how unhealthy this climate can be for a man from Texas. See that he understands how wise it would be to keep moving. If he isn't receptive to that idea, he should disappear. Get my drift?"

Stone Wolf gave a dark nod.

"You want some help, take Patch and Worthy with you."

The Indian stood and walked to the door, turned and spat on the floor, contemptuous at the suggestion he might need the help of Blaine's fumbling gun toters. His leave-taking was but a whisper in the night.

Stone Wolf lay hidden atop a ragged bluff overlooking the Flying M. He watched with little interest as Court Blaine escorted Linda Macklin from the house to the elegant carriage. The gambler helped the girl onto the upholstered bench, walked around the back of the vehicle and, climbing in beside her, flicked the reins. The black mare started at a prance and they headed from the ranchyard bound for Raindance.

Stone Wolf had no intention of trying to persuade or threaten the new Flying M ramrod to leave the territory. He wanted the appaloosa for his own, and he planned to carry off whatever else of value he could find on the ranch. It would be a simple thing to kill this Boone Smith, ransack the buildings, then dispose of the foreman's body. He pulled a rifle from its fringed and beaded buckskin case and settled down to wait and watch.

The dusky killer's head came up as the front door of the ranchhouse swung open. He raised his rifle, placed the cool, smooth stock against his cheek and squeezed off his shot.

On this evening, Dancer was astride the blood bay he used as a pack horse and occasional remount, giving the appaloosa a well-deserved rest. Jack had spent the afternoon on the range checking the cattle and was headed back to the ranchhouse as he heard the wild complaint of a ricocheted bullet. Even while the angry whine of the rifle shot lingered around him, Dancer urged the big, black-maned horse beneath him into a ground-eating run, unleathering his Henry as he rode.

As he neared ranch headquarters, two more shots rang out. Two separate rifles. Dancer pointed the bay into the trees, approaching the battle scene under cover.

Macklin knelt at the window inside the spacious front room of the ranchhouse, rifle in hand, his face covered with a dozen bleeding punctures. The first sniping shot from atop the bluff had barely missed his head, striking the door jamb and showering him with splinters. He had reacted swiftly, lunging back inside, and had scrambled to get his rifle from the rack of guns on the north wall. Now he was engaged in an exchange of pot shots with whoever was out there. The rancher thought of Dancer, hoped he would be alerted by the shooting, not come riding in unaware.

Dancer listened to the sporadic rifle fire, locating the source of the attack as the bluff to the east of the ranch. He loosely tied his horse in the trees, heading upslope through the thick stand of conifers. Wishing he had his moccasins, Jack made his way through the forest with as much stealth as possible. More shots. He was close now. He dropped behind a fallen pine and eased himself carefully toward the ledge from which the sniper fire was coming. He laid his rifle aside and palmed his sixgun, then peered over the log.

Nothing!

The shooter had disappeared. Dancer lay motionless, searching the surrounding cover for movement. Still nothing. He got cautiously to his feet and eased forward to the bluff. Whoever had been there had ghosted away and was out of sight. He walked to the spot of ambush and looked at the ground, then stopped to pick up a spent brass cartridge, .44 caliber. There were six of the casings scattered about. He pocketed the one he held in his hand, noted where the man had lain in wait, then spotted the footprints. Moccasin tracks, same as he had noticed in the woods where he found Hawkes.

Dancer walked to the edge of the bluff and waved his hat back and forth as a signal of all clear to Macklin, inside the ranchhouse. He did not hear the sharp report as the Indian's shot sent his body plummeting over the edge.

Linda Macklin's smile flashed with the radiance of sun off a high mountain lake as the courtly gambler led her off the dance floor to their small table. She was thoroughly enjoying herself, grateful for this respite from the pressures of the situation at the ranch.

Blaine had proved to be a most charming escort. He was a witty and entertaining conversationalist, and graceful on the dance floor. And he was, after all, quite a handsome man. Court was impeccably attired, as usual, in a tailored, black broadcloth, three-piece suit, gray linen shirt, gray silk pocket handkerchief, black tie and gray hat. When he unlimbered his winning smile, you could hear female sighs all over the crowded hall, emanating from the hopeful debutantes of Raindance.

Nor was Linda to be outshone by her natty escort. She was breathtaking in a blue satin gown, her blond hair cascading in long, loose curls over smooth, golden shoulders. Her blue eyes were sparkling, sassy and alive. She was notably the most ravishing of the beauties at the ball.

The ladies of the community whispered, gossiped and giggled as they forecast the future of the handsome couple. It is not a great distance from first date to altar in the collective minds and imaginations of sewing circles in any town, Raindance not excepted.

The annual spring dance was an eagerly awaited affair in the small community, and its occurrence drew celebrants from miles around. Townsfolk, farmers, ranchhands, lumberjacks, miners and their women had been drawn together by the common need for diversion from lives of struggle and hardship. The hall was gaily strung with colorful banners of bunting. Long tables were laden with prepared foods of every description, prized recipes brought in covered dishes by ladies seeking some measure of recognition for their efforts. Gay refrains from fiddle, guitar, Jew's harp and mouth organ filled the hall, competing with the chatter and laughter of good people at fun.

Court Blaine, as with gamblers in many places across the frontier, was a respected member of this small community. He ran a straight game, mostly, despite Quint Hawkes' biased, jealousy-tainted opinion. His skill did not require him to cheat at gambling, though he was certainly adept at it, and would if circumstances warranted it. But Blaine's ambitions were on a loftier plane than low-stake card games. He aimed for far greater wealth than could be had by sleight of hand. He wanted his gold.

Blaine had said nothing this night about the ranch. He would wait until he heard from Stone Wolf. Then, when her back was against the wall, he would make Linda an offer for her property. A generous gesture made by a caring man, a friend. Tonight's escort duty was merely to serve as enjoyable groundwork laid toward his ultimate goal.

Suddenly a young man burst into the hall, breathless and excited, his clothing in dusty disarray. All heads turned to watch as he scanned the gathered celebrants. He spotted Linda, paused to gather his wind and his courage, and ran toward her.

"Miss Macklin! You remember me? I'm George Beeson, done some work for your pa. I just come from out your way, ma'am. The Flying M is on fire!"

Excitement carried on rising voices throughout the gathering. People hurried to saddle their mounts and hitch their teams to wagons and buggies, then followed Blaine and Linda in a reckless, pellmell rush to the ranch. The night sky ahead of the racing caravan was tinted a ghastly orange glow, the moon eradicated by billowing columns of smoke.

By the time the wagons, carriages and horsemen came clattering into the Flying M yard amid the din of jangling trace chains, the slap of leather reins, whinnies and whoas, the ranchhouse had been reduced to an ugly heap of blackened, smoldering rubble, blazing now in just a few scattered spots. Only the flame-scarred hitchrail remained standing, looking like a blistered specter mocking the dismayed onlookers. The bunkhouse, too, lay in smoking ruin. Intense heat kept everyone well back from the site, appalled and helpless.

Linda leaped from the buggy, tears coursing down her cheeks. She ran toward the charred remnants of her home, screaming, "No! No! Oh, my God, no!"

Court Blaine caught her by the shoulders and drew the sobbing, distraught young woman to his chest. He felt a momentary twinge of pity, then realizing what the tragedy meant to his plan, allowed himself an unseen smile.

Chapter Nine

Macklin had seen Dancer stagger when shot and fall, bouncing crazily like a sack of oats, down the steep slope of the bluff. He watched Stone Wolf creep to the rim, peer at his handiwork, then with a glimpse toward the ranch, draw back from view. Undoubtedly headed for the ranchhouse to finish his chore of destruction and murder. Knowing he hadn't a moment to lose, the rancher grabbed his rifle, took a shotgun from the rack on the wall, strapped on a sidearm, filled his pockets with ammunition and rushed into the bedroom. Hawkes was standing, stooped and clutching his wound, a confused and wondering look on his face.

"Let's get you dressed, Quint. We've got to get out of here, now—or we're both going to be murdered again. This time for real."

He started to help his foreman into his pants. Hawkes insisted that he could manage, so Macklin gathered a few food goods in an empty flour sack, deposited it on the back stoop, then ran for the corral. He did not take the time to saddle the horses, just slipped hackamores over their noses and trotted them back to the house. Hawkes was leaning against the kitchen door jamb when he got there. Macklin hoisted the cowboy onto the broad back of a big sorrel, grabbed the sack and guns and crawled clumsily off the step onto his own horse. With Hawkes lying low on the horse's neck, they galloped away into the gnarled camouflage of the forest west of the ranch, just as Stone Wolf eased his horse out of the trees on the other side of the valley, his view of the escaping horsemen blocked by the ranchhouse.

They rode aimlessly, deeper into the timber and climbing steadily, gripped by the fear of pursuit. Suddenly racked by pain, Hawkes slid off the side of his lathered mount, landing heavily with a whoosh of breath and a grunt on the needle-cushioned floor of the forest. Macklin jumped from his horse to rush to his friend's aid.

"Just lie there and rest," he said after making the wounded cowhand as comfortable as he could.

"I don't think we're being followed. I have to go back."

"Go back? You crazy, boss, or just tired of living?"

"Neither I hope, my friend. I've just taken time to think. I was in such an all-fired hurry to save my own hide and yours, I didn't give a thought to Jack Dancer."

"But he's dead, Rad. You seen him go down yourself. They ain't nothin' you can do for him now."

"Probably, but I have to be sure. The man put his life on the line for us. All of us. I owe him.

"If you feel up to it later, Quint, make your way to that cave where me and Linda holed up before. Nobody's likely to find you there. I'll check on Dancer first, then come back here. If you're gone, I'll meet you at the cave."

With that, Macklin mounted and rode watchfully back toward the Flying M.

When Stone Wolf found no one in the house, he looted the place room by room and packed his plunder onto his own horse, switching his saddle to Jack Dancer's side-stepping, complaining appaloosa. Sloshing coal oil from lamps onto the walls and floors, the predatory Comanche set the fire. Moving to the bunkhouse, he ransacked it, finding nothing of value, then set that structure afire as well.

The Indian was puzzled as to who the rifleman in the house had been and where he had gotten to. But there was no time to investigate. He would let Blaine worry about that. The fire from the ranchhouse already illuminated the landscape, casting weird, flickering reflections off the low-hanging clouds. Night was falling rapidly. The fire's glow would be noticed by any chance passerby. Stone Wolf would not tarry to find, bury or hide the foreman's body. To do so would be to chance discovery. Smiling wickedly, he mounted the stolen stallion, took the lead of his pack animal in hand and rode away up the valley.

Macklin rode cautiously from the woods toward the blazing ranchhouse, dreading what he would find. He had seen the glow of the fire from further back and knew more or less what to expect. Still, the sight of the blazing inferno that had been his hard-earned home hit him like the blow of a hard-swung shovel blade to the stomach. Grim-faced, he circled the burning buildings, pausing at the corral to take a saddle and bridle from off the top rail. He saddled up, then went at a lope to the base of the bluff where he had seen Dancer fall. Pausing often to glance over his shoulder, Macklin searched the underbrush at the foot of the steep slope, now hampered by darkness. No body. Maybe the Indian had disposed of it to hide his crime. He continued to prowl the brush for half an hour. He kicked something in the weeds and bent to pick up a handgun, easily recognized as one of the matched pair belonging to his friend. But he could find no clue as to the fate of Jack Dancer.

Linda sat stiffly on the edge of the bed in her hotel room, anxious and dejected, unable to sleep for worrying, not knowing what to do or to whom she could turn.

There had been no bodies found in the burned ruin of the

house. Was her father dead? And Quint Hawkes? What of Dancer? *What had happened?* Linda was certain the fire had not been an accident. Her mind raced with questions to which she had no hint of answers. Tomorrow she must get a horse and ride out there, see if she might find anything that could possibly give her direction.

Perhaps, if she was to confide in him, Court Blaine could help.

Dawn crept hesitantly into the valley, its customary brilliance held in check by thick, low clouds that obscured the upper slopes. Faint low growls of thunder hinted of the storm brewing amid the mountain peaks far to the west.

Impelled by thirst, the blood bay, left loosely tethered in the forest the previous evening, had pulled free its reins to forage the meadow of the valley floor, pausing now to graze, then wandering on. As the big animal neared the base of the bluff it sniffed the breeze and pricked forward its ears. Following its alerted senses, it came to stand over the motionless form of Jack Dancer, lying hidden in the shallow, weed-choked depression of a dry creek bed.

Snorting at the dread stench of blood, the horse backed away, pawing at the ground and shaking its massive head. The familiar man smell coaxed it back. It nuzzled at the face of the still figure. Its master moved.

Dancer lay swaddled in black silence. Slowly, stupidly, he opened his eyes. The somber, cloud-diffused light of dawn assaulted him and he squeezed his eyes tight shut again. Awareness advanced grudgingly into his swimming brain. Where was he? What had happened? Again he forced open his eyes, fighting the throbbing explosions in his skull. Something had struck him, knocking him over the ledge. A bullet. He was wounded then, and he had taken a fall. Carefully he began testing his muscles. Tears welled in his eyes as each injury brutally made itself known.

Jack tried to sit and was slammed back by the pain. He tried once more, steeling himself against the hurt, coming slowly to a sitting position. His head spun wildly. He steadied himself. The wounded man's side was drenched with blood, the source of the flow high up under his left arm. The bullet had entered his back, tearing through muscle, glanced off a rib and exited his chest under the left breast. He hoped the broken rib had not punctured his lung. He thought not, though breathing was agonizingly difficult.

God, he was thirsty. Due to a loss of blood, he assumed. His canteen hung tantalizingly from the saddle on the black-maned bay. He would need to get to his feet to reach it. The mere thought of expending the effort to do that was depressing.

Dancer tenderly explored his limbs for broken bones. He found none, but lordy, he was sore. The fall had left him covered head to foot with bruises, scrapes, cuts and scratches, oftentimes more painful and bothersome than shattered bones.

He leaned to reach the trailing reins of the big horse, grateful now for his uncommon practice of making pets of his riding stock. Then he began the painful transition to a standing position. Each movement was an exercise in torture. Each breath a torment. Sweat poured forth on his forehead in the cool morning air. Using the stirrups and saddle rigging, Dancer scaled the heaving side of the skittish horse, inch by grueling inch.

Finally, he stood erect. Dancer drank, rested, then drank again.

The gun was missing from its holster at Jack's waist, but its mate was in the saddlebag on the horse. He fished it out and leathered it, hooking the rawhide loop over the hammer.

He would need his rifle. If his unseen assailant had not discovered it, the weapon would still be in the woods where he had cached it the evening before. Slowly and purposeful-ly, he forced his screaming body into the saddle.

When Dancer looked toward the ranchyard and saw the steaming rubble, his heart leaped into his throat. Had Macklin and Hawkes escaped, or did their bodies lie charred in the ruins, caught in the holocaust? He started the horse easily, holding it to a walk.

As he passed the smith's shed, Dancer stared angrily at the empty corral. The bushwhacking sonofagun was sitting his prize stallion.

"Hope he bites your back-shootin' trigger finger off," he muttered to himself.

Following a fruitless search of the ashes for signs of his friends' remains, Jack retrieved his rifle and headed the bay upslope. Before any other consideration, he had to find a safe place to hole up, to dress his wounds and get some rest. He wanted to sleep for a week.

Remembering the ramshackle trapper's cabin where he had stayed earlier, Dancer headed in that direction. The arduous journey through dense forest and brush over rocky and rugged terrain seemed to him to last forever. Several times he snapped awake, still in the saddle, having been either asleep or unconscious. As dusk crept into the moun-tains, the bedraggled rider, at last, reached the cabin. His wound was bleeding, he was feverish, he was exhausted to the point of tears. Turning the bay into the corral, Jack dis-mounted, stumbling to his knees. Using the stirrups, he pulled himself up again, loosed the cinch to let the saddle slip to the turf then, dragging his saddlebags and bedroll, limped and staggered to the cabin.

Dancer forced himself to build a fire and to heat water for his wounds. He stripped off his shirt, grimacing at the hot reminders of his torn flesh.

"Jack, boy," he grumbled grimly while surveying a body

scarred by a variety of old wounds, "you've collected more plugged holes in your hide than a shotgunned jackrabbit."

When he had cleansed the worst of the cuts and the bullet wound, Dancer dressed them as best he could. He laboriously rolled a cigarette—a recent, seldom-practiced habit—and lay down to smoke.

Outside, the bay turned its rump to the northwest and crowded close to the side of the dilapidated shack that served as one side of the ancient corral. The night that loomed above the forest dwarfed the trees, and the towering conifers began to sway, quake and bow to the belligerent gusts like stringy-haired aborigines in a peyote-fired frenzy, dancing and dipping to nature's most ancient ritual.

A crash of thunder that shook the rocks for miles around split the early night, the angry report causing the manhunter to jerk violently. Then the roar of heavy rain bucketing onto the roof brought a smile to his lips. The downpour would cover his tracks.

He crushed out the ugly butt of the clumsily fashioned cigarette on the tamped earthen floor and lay down, pulling the blanket, one-handed, up to his ears.

Gratefully, Dancer closed his eyes.

Caleb Free was a hideous sight. The front half of his skull was covered with ugly, gleaming scar tissue where the Utes had scalped him. The bullet that had plowed through his jaw left the lower half of his face terribly puckered and gnarled, so that now he spoke from a tiny, obscene aperture on his left cheek.

When the war party swooped down on the Blackthorn gang's camp in the canyon, Caleb Free, gravely wounded, had played dead, lying without struggle as the Ute buck standing astride him ripped the scalp from his head with a sickening, sucking sound.

With spots gamboling before his eyes, Free had seen Jubal

Blackthorn and Court Blaine emerge from the brush, where the pair had fled to escape the attack, lugging their personal saddlebags in their arms. Free attempted to call to them, but the feeble, animalistic sounds he made through his wounds went unheard.

Focused on his own agony, Caleb had watched with pre-occupied interest as Court Blaine plunged a knife into his leader's back. He had lain witness as the turncoat bandit put a bullet between the bewildered and disbelieving eyes of Jubal Blackthorn.

After Blaine had skulked away into the trees, Caleb Free made his way over the bodies of his comrades, all of them scalped, many of their corpses savagely mutilated. He dazedly entered the dense forest. He struggled through the hostile wilderness, stumbling and crawling, living off plump grubs and berries and writhing vermin, swallowing the disgusting fare whole because his wound would not allow him to chew.

Finally, near death and with the will to survive depleted, Caleb had been found by a woodsman, who took him to an Indian squaw, a spirit woman. Almost a year he stayed with the squaw, accepting her ministrations, incantations, pagan spells and herbal medications before regaining his health.

Now, after more years of aimlessly wandering the raw frontier, Caleb Free was sitting in a card game at the Golconda Saloon in Raindance. His face twisted beyond its physical mutilation with hatred, he looked across the room at a smiling, dapper Court Blaine. The gambler had looked directly at him, right into his scarred and misshapen features, and that backstabber Blaine had not recognized him.

As his hands tightened into fists, crumpling his full house of jacks over fives, Caleb Free grinned hideously, his grotesque mouth askew. Jubal Blackthorn had been the youngest of four brothers in a close-knit, feudal family.

Caleb reckoned the surviving Blackthorn boys would be mighty interested in the whereabouts of Jubal's jaunty assassin.

Linda's face was smudged with soot, the hem of her dress soiled black from shuffling through the ashes of the ranch-house ruins. The agony of endless hopes followed by despairs marked her wandering progress among the remains of all her possessions. Rivulets of tears left harlequin streaks of white against her blackened cheeks. Court Blaine offered his silk handkerchief as he stepped mincingly through the debris to avoid mussing his wardrobe.

"Let me take you back to town, my dear. There is nothing here for you now."

She nodded. "I just hoped there might be some sign . . ."

Linda abruptly clamped her lips into a tight, white line, having almost let slip that her father had been in the house. Where was he? And Dancer, and poor Quint? Were they all dead? Was she alone? No, she could not allow herself to believe that—she would not believe it. She vowed to search until she found the answer.

"Let's go back to town, please, Court. I want to change into my riding clothes. I need to ride out, to be alone for a while."

"Of course, whatever you wish.

"It's quite evident to me, Linda, what happened here. This man you hired, this Boone Smith, must have looted your house, packed the valuables on the horses, then burned the ranch to hide his crime. He is probably halfway to Texas or Mexico by now. Don't you agree?"

Hardly listening, Linda merely shrugged, then stepped into the carriage. She thought as they rode back toward Raindance that if she should fail to find the missing men by her own efforts today, she must enlist the gambler's help. To do that, of course, would necessitate revealing to him that her father was, or had been, still alive. It was a risk to confide in anyone, but what else could she do?

Meanwhile, miles away, a rifle shot reverberated through a canyon. A doe took two soaring leaps, then fell dead, a bullet in its heart. Rad Macklin made his way cautiously toward the carcass of the deer, scanning the surrounding landscape as he crept stealthily through the brush. There always existed the danger that a shot would be heard by enemies, but they had to eat. The few supplies he had brought from the ranch would not last long for two grown men, and they needed meat. Hawkes was improving daily, so they should be able to move on soon, but for now it was better that they remain secreted in the cave.

The rancher skillfully skinned the deer and cut away the choice portions, bundled them in the hide and slung it over his shoulder. He picked up his rifle with his free hand and started back to the hideaway.

Rad was worried about Linda. She was no doubt safe enough in town or on the ranch of friends, but he knew that she would be frantic with worry and confused as to what to do. His daughter was a level-headed girl, sure, but she had never been forced to deal with this sort of trouble. He hoped she was up to it, that she was keeping her own counsel. If only Dancer had not been killed.

Macklin struggled up the slope to the ledge in front of the cave and, with a weary grunt, swung his burden to the stone floor. He paused to catch his breath, grumbled something concerning advancing age, then leaned his gun against the bundle of venison and stepped into the cavern to check on Quint Hawkes.

Apparently asleep, Hawkes was lying on his side, back to the opening, a flickering candle alight on the rock shelf above him. Macklin crossed to shake him awake.

"Well now, howdy there, boss. Fancy seein' you here, back from the dead and all."

Macklin whipped his head around toward the voice. Patch and Worthy stood, grinning, the evil black bores of their outlaw guns trained on his chest.

Chapter Ten

For four days Dancer tossed and raved in delirium, his clothing soaked with sweat, alternately burning with fever and quaking with chills. A heavy film hindered his eyesight. Strange visions clouded his brain, ominous shadows lurked in the corners of the cabin. Once, in a brief moment of lucidity, he thought he heard horses pass in the nearby pines, and the muffled voices of riders, but he saw nothing from the dirt-hazed window, and then the sounds were gone.

The days passed slowly, great chunks of time to be endured. But the manhunter forced himself to eat and to rest, knowing both were vital to his rapid recovery. At first, the slightest movement exhausted him. By the end of a week he was able to move about, stiffly and painfully at first, then eventually without much discomfort.

The horse had fared well on the grass growing in the ancient corral. Rain had filled a rocky depression at the back of the rail enclosure, so the bay had not suffered during its master's period of infirmity.

A nearby stream offered a plentiful supply of fat trout and

good water, and as the days passed Dancer was able to venture into the surrounding woods for game.

Dancer was a rugged young man, game as a bear dog and hardened by years of rigorous living in the myriad mountain wildernesses of the Rockies, facing the challenges of an untamed frontier that demanded strength and purpose to roam its vast reaches. The clean mountain air, plenty of food and rest, combined with his natural resiliency and strength of will, served to promote the healing of his wounds and to escalate the restoration of health, strength and vitality to his battered body. By the middle of the second week following his run-in with Stone Wolf, he was packing to leave.

The tendons in Dancer's neck grew as taut as telegraph wires as a simmering fury began to build in his gut. To this point he had been playing it pretty cozy, looking for motives for the attacks on Macklin, waiting for something to happen before he acted. Well, no more. Now he intended to extend a strenuous hospitality to anyone who crossed his path. He would hide no more from the patchwork law in Raindance. Dancer was going on the hunt. It was time for action. Time to attack!

"Should we kill 'em?"

The light from the flickering candle cast Patch's hunched vulture shadow on the cavern wall.

"Yeah, I reckon. That was the original orders. Why? You think we'd ought to check it out with the man first?"

"Mightn't be a bad idea. You mind how testy he gets when we go off and do somethin' on our own."

"Why don't you tend 'em, then, while I ride in to town and check it out?"

"Yeah, all right. Bring back a bottle when you come. I'm so dry I'm a dadgum fire hazard."

Worthy crouched as he walked from the cave. Moments

later, the tattoo of a horse's hooves could be heard disappearing down the mountain toward Raindance.

Patch slid down the stone wall to a sitting position. He smiled at his captives as he rolled a smoke one-handed, keeping his sixgun trained on Rad Macklin and Quint Hawkes.

"What's this all about, Patch?" Macklin asked. "Who's paying you? Who's behind all this?"

"Wouldn't do you no good to know, old man," the outlaw replied, then shifted his attention to the foreman.

"Y'know, Hawkes, I'm pleasured to see you still kickin'. Does my ol' heart good to see as how that scary Indian ain't so stinkin' mean as he thinks he is. He just knowed you was a goner when he cut you. Ha! Kind of makes up for my messin' up the killin' of Macklin, here."

A wild notion struck Hawkes. He had noticed while working with Patch that the man was uncommonly superstitious.

"Why Virgil, what made you think we're both not dead? You never seen a ghost before?"

A wild look of sudden, fearful doubt flashed into the gunman's eyes. The cigarette fell from his lips to his lap. He jumped up, flustered, swatting at the live ashes. Both Hawkes and Macklin lunged for him at once.

They rolled on the ground grunting, grappling and groaning, a tumbling tangle of arms and legs. Patch's gun discharged, filling the musty, confined cavity of the cave with gunsmoke and the stifling smell of brimstone, the report magnified and ringing in the ears of the desperate combatants. The struggling slowed, then stopped.

Macklin and Hawkes lay back, panting.

Virgil Patch did not move. A dark, widening stain soaked his plaid shirt, coloring the round tag that hung from the punctured tobacco sack in his chest pocket like the red of a setting sun.

The two friends looked at each other, exhausted, frightened, not quite realizing what had occurred. Then they began to laugh.

"Let's make tracks out of here."

"You stupid bunglers!"

Court Blaine was livid. He stood astraddle the stiffening form of his dead hireling, screaming with uncontrollable rage into the unhearing corpse's grainy white face, now puffy in death like overcooked rice. Spittle flew from his bellowing lips as he raved.

Blaine whirled, backhanding an abashed and cowering Worthy across the mouth, drawing blood and knocking the hired gunman sprawling across the floor of the cave. Manfred Worthy began, in reflex action, to draw his gun. The madness in the larger man's eyes stayed his hand.

"Can't you idiots do anything right? You ride all the way into town to tell me that Macklin and Hawkes are both alive . . . then your bumbling partner lets them escape!"

"Now wait a minute," Worthy said, wiping the blood from his split lip. "It don't look to me as if this was all ol' Patch's idea. You was tellin' me how good we done until we got here and found them gone."

"Shut up. Let me think."

Blaine stormed through the mouth of the cave to the ledge. Worthy hesitated, then followed along in a sullen pout, rubbing his jaw.

"This has gone on long enough. I want it ended. Go get Stone Wolf. I want both of you in my quarters as soon as it's dark. Do you think you might be capable of handling a big chore like that?"

"Yeah, I can handle that," Worthy replied tersely. His features stiffened and he stared coldly through slitted lids into the gambler's eyes.

"And Blaine," he warned, "don't ever lay hands on me again. I'll kill you."

The sun was sucking up red, orange and purple wisps of clouds in the west as Jack Dancer and the big blood bay mincingly picked their way along the narrow lip of a trail around a granite bluff halfway up the canyon wall. As the rider rounded a bulging boulder, he pulled the horse to a halt. A few feet ahead, the edge of the trail had fallen away, the exposed earth of the scar still damp. Upon closer examination, Dancer could detect scuff marks in the dirt where a traveler had evidently scrambled frantically to avoid falling. Carefully and slowly he eased out of the saddle and sidled forward for a closer look. He peered over the edge to the rocky floor of the rift, more than a hundred feet below. There lay a body, grotesquely twisted, unmoving. From this vantage point and in the gathering gloom, it appeared to be a young Indian boy. He could not tell if he was dead.

Darkness had crept into the canyon by the time Dancer bottomed out at the base of the cliff. He unsaddled the bay, staking it on the edge of a grove of poplar where the grasses grew high and sweet. Then, bundling together dead boughs of fir as a makeshift torch, he set about to locate the ill-fated traveler who had fallen from the heights.

The crumpled form lying tangled among the rock proved, indeed, to be an Indian boy. Ute, the manhunter surmised by his costume and features, and he was alive.

The lad was unconscious, his left leg badly broken, the shattered bone glaring stark and white where it protruded through the russet flesh. Further examination satisfied Dancer that the young Ute had no discernible internal injuries, though he had been badly bruised and battered as he bounced and careened against the unforgiving stone cliff walls. Dancer identified closely with the boy's condition and he fingered his own recent, still tender injuries in remembrance. Still, this was a mighty lucky little Indian. Dead leaves and debris had blown and gathered to a considerable depth within the cluster of boulders where he had landed, cushioning the impact of his plunge and saving his life.

Leaving the unconscious boy where he lay, Dancer crossed the field of rocks to a level, grassy stretch beside the babbling stream that dissected the length of the canyon. He built a fire, put water to heat and spread a blanket by the crackling flames to receive the injured youth.

After he had cleansed the ugly wounds, Dancer set and splinted the young Indian's shattered leg as best he could, grateful that the boy remained unaware throughout the rigorous procedure. Then, tired and hungry, he ate some cold smoked meat, washing it down with a pot of black, bitter coffee. Checking to make sure his charge was resting comfortably, Dancer rolled into his own blankets. He stared up at the thin strip of star-speckled indigo sky between the black canyon walls.

The manhunter expelled a frustrated sigh. He was anxious to be on the trail of Stone Wolf, and to put the entire puzzling Macklin matter behind him. Now he had saddled himself with a crippled youngster. A delay of unpredictable duration was inevitable. Being the sort of man he was, Jack Dancer could consider no other course. He slept.

A week passed at the camp in the canyon as Dancer nursed the boy, an alert youngster in his early teens. Although not fluent in the Ute tongue, Dancer did speak Shoshoni, and the Utes were linguistically and culturally related to their Shoshoni cousins of the north. Combining those bits of knowledge with sign language, the white man was able to communicate. He learned that the lad's name was Fire Cloud, and that he was the son of Four Feathers, a chieftain of the Ute Mountain Indians, and grandson to Ouray.

Dancer knew of old Chief Ouray, Fire Cloud's famous grandfather and the man for whom the town of Ouray was named. He had been the undisputed leader of all the Utes a few years back, revered and feared by his people and a great friend to the white man. The chief had chosen to join the whites rather than fight them, motivated in part by his fondness for the white way of life. He often hosted dinners and feasts, plying his guests with wine and cigars furnished him by officers of the US Army. While the chiefs of other tribes puffed on *kinnikinick*, an aromatic mixture of tobacco leaves and the dried bark of the red willow, Ouray relaxed with a fine cigar from the stores of the white man. He'd been an iron-willed autocrat, single-handedly keeping his militant band under control by shooting all opponents of his peaceful policies. His firm control went uncontested until 1872, when he signed away a large parcel of tribal land. Other tribal leaders were mystified and chagrined as to Ouray's motives. What benefit would the people realize by the ceding of tribal lands? Later, the Utes found out that the wily chief had been rewarded with a government stipend of $1,000 a year for life. Stripped of omnipotence, Ouray nonetheless continued as a strong influence in tribal affairs and retained his status as Chief of the Uncompahgre Utes, Fire Cloud's band, until his death in 1880, when his son, Four Feathers, became chief.

Jack also knew that Utes were involved in the last great Indian battle in Colorado—the Thornburgh Massacre, in 1878. Unhappy with their assigned lives on the reservation land the whites had forced upon them, the Utes had ambushed Federal troops. Jack did not know if Ouray's band had been involved in the battle, and felt it prudent not to ask.

Fire Cloud told the white man that he had come into the mountains alone to face his ritual of trial, fasting and meditation, preparatory to becoming a full-fledged brave. The Indian boy was grateful to Dancer for his Samaritan care and attention, but was most anxious to return to his village on the reservation to the southwest. Dancer warned that such a journey would surely prove to be painfully taxing, but Fire Cloud insisted that he must go. Impatient to be about his own affairs, Jack reluctantly agreed, and the two new friends made preparations to depart the following morning.

Dancer was mounted on the bay at first light, heading downcanyon in search of an easier route to the top. The day's journey promised to be difficult enough for both him and the boy without hauling a litter up the precipitous, narrow trail from which Fire Cloud had fallen. He found a suitable alternative and by noon had fashioned a travois to which he secured the injured youth with cloth strips cut from a blanket. The trek to the top was long and winding. When the pair stopped for the night they were still within sight of their previous evening's camp, two hundred feet below them. Four days later they paused atop a rise to look down upon the lodges of the Uncompahgre Ute.

The reputation of Jack Dancer preceded him onto the Ute reservation. They knew him as a great warrior, who was of the lodge of John Dancer, friend to the Cherokee, the Kiowa, the Nez Perce and Shoshoni. The account of the pair's relentless pursuit of the killers, the McCabes, had reached the ears of the Ute. Jack Dancer had become a legend, of sorts, for his fierceness and valor in the battle in the cliff city of the Ancient Ones. Known, too, for his tracking prowess, and for his conquest in conflicts with many foes—some of whom were enemies of the Ute, as well. The hunter of men was received as a hero among the lodges of the tribe. A great feast would be held in his honor, with Chief Four Feathers holding sway over the festivities.

A roaring bonfire brightly lit a large, circular area in the center of the Ute village. Every member of the tribe from tiniest papoose to the most ancient of the elders, gathered to pay homage to the rescuer of the chief's son. Ringing the ceremonial ground, brown bodies moved in rhythm to the primeval beat of the drums.

Chief Four Feathers sat in regal dignity at the station of honor, his legs folded, his outstretched arms held palms down on his knees, back as rigid as a lodgepole. His robes were of the finest buckskin, laboriously chewed soft by the teeth of Ute squaws, fringed and intricately beaded in colorful and symbolic patterns. His straight, black hair hung in braids to his waist. A gold ring dangled from his right ear, and he wore a gold wedding band on his left hand in the manner of the white man, an affectation borrowed from his father, Ouray. Beaded necklaces and amulets were draped around his neck. Four Feathers' countenance was stern and somber, and any man who looked upon him must surely know at once that, like his famous father before him, the man was indeed a chief among his people.

Indicative of the honor bestowed upon him, Jack Dancer sat to the chief's right with his legs folded, arms at ease in his lap. To his father's left sat a proud and smiling Fire Cloud, his splinted leg extended stiffly in front of him.

The pageantry unfolded. Lithe young warriors bedecked in colorful ceremonial finery, their supple and muscular bodies greased and gleaming in the firelight, danced gracefully to the savage beat of the drums. Headdresses of porcupine guard hairs and deer tails became animated by the gyrations. Each movement of their pounding, stamping, moccasined feet generated a primitive musical accompaniment from the bands of deer toes jangling on their legs. The audience stomped and chanted and clapped in perfect rhythmic participation as the fervor of the handsome dancers intensified.

Dancer watched in appreciation, his interest increasing as young Ute maidens took their turn at the dancing.

The spectacle continued for hours with much singing of prayers and songs and the telling of tales. The ceremonial climax of the evening made Dancer, Hunter of Men, an honorary Ute, blood brother to Four Feathers and Fire Cloud. This solemn gesture was an honor rarely accorded a white man and Dancer respected it as such.

"Brothers, my heart is happy that you accept this white man into the society of the mighty Ute. All men know of the strength and bravery of your warriors. The wisdom of your chiefs is storied near and far. No tribe can match the cunning and skill of the Ute. I am proud. The strength of my limbs will be doubled, for now I am Ute. My heart will be as brave as ten men, for now I am Ute. My spirit soars with the eagle, because I am Ute.

"My lodge is your lodge from this day. My weapons are poised to slay the enemies of my brothers. I must leave you with the rising of the sun, but the spirit of the man called Dancer shall remain among the lodges of the Ute, for you are my people.

"May all your days be filled with plenty. May your horses run swiftly, your arrows fly true. May the cooking pots of your lodges be always full. May no squaw's tears be shed in mourning. May the Great Spirit be with you, my people, forever."

Chapter Eleven

"**K**idnap a *woman?* You just gone crazy here lately, or was you *born* off plumb?"

Worthy was dumbstruck. He could not believe the outlandish plan that his employer was proposing.

"Why, a man so much as looks crossways at a woman in this country, he's buzzard bait. We get caught at this here, they'll hang us head down over a slow fire. No, no, no!"

His strident objection brought the gunman a look from Blaine that could cure head lice.

"Quit your blasted blubbering and listen for once, Worthy. You do this like I tell you, exactly like I tell you, there is no way you will be found out.

"Here's how it's going to go. Miss Macklin has consented to accompany me for a ride in the country this evening. We will be in my rig. You both know it when you see it, right?"

Stone Wolf and Worthy gestured positively.

"I'll drive southeast on the old Bent's Fort trail to Blanca Creek, where there is a field of wildflowers. The lady is fond of flowers.

"That's where you jump us. Bring a horse for her to ride.

I want you both to wear masks, and you should not talk more than you have to.

"Stone Wolf, I'll act as though I'm going to put up a struggle. You pretend to knock me unconscious. Be careful, but make it look good. Then you grab the girl. There is a shack up by Devil's Head where we often used to lay low when I was riding with Blackthorn. It is well stocked and well hidden. Take her there."

"I hope you do not plan that the woman come back," the breed said.

"No . . . she won't be coming back."

"Then why don't we just kill her right off?" Worthy asked.

"Let me explain. I want that ranch, and I want it with clear deed to the property. That means Macklin must sign it over to me. He is aware, after the incident at the cave, that we know he is alive . . . so he is going to realize he has nothing to gain by remaining hidden. Sooner or later, and I figure sooner, he will come to town looking for his daughter. When he does, I've got him hogtied.

"I tell him that Linda is our captive, that the only way he is ever to see her alive again is to sign over the Flying M to me. I will promise him that once I have the paper, that I will lead him to his daughter."

Worthy rolled his eyes back in his head, convinced that the plan was the most stupid thing he had yet heard.

"I know, I know," Blaine said, "he's not a fool. He will know that we plan to kill them both, but what else can he do? He will have no choice. I'll bring him to the hideout, then we will finish it. It's foolproof, men, I guarantee it."

"That still don't tell us why the girl is got to stay alive," Worthy argued. "He won't know no different 'til you drag him out there . . . then it'll be too late."

"She is insurance, just in case I may be forced to kill Rad

Macklin before he puts his name to that deed. She is his legal heir. If anything should happen, I will force her to sign it."

The two surly hirelings looked at each other apprehensively.

"You tell us why you put on an act for the girl if she is to die. Why make like you are protecting her from us?" asked Stone Wolf.

"Simple. If you two botch it somehow, yours truly is going to be in the clear. I am simply hedging my bet, boys. You blame me, the way things have gone up to now?"

A spark of realization kindled a gleam in Manfred Worthy's eyes.

"You are lookin' to get rich out of this deal somehow, Blaine. You don't give a hoot for any ranch. There's money in this somewheres . . . and we want in. Right, Stone Wolf?"

The Indian nodded his agreement.

"Why, sure thing, boys. I hope you didn't think for a minute that I would leave you out of this. You have my promise. You'll both get what you deserve."

Six grave men came riding.

Three abreast rode the Blackthorn boys, on big, highstepping chestnut geldings. The eldest, Peaceable John, held the center position, riding just a hair ahead of his brothers, Jacob and Jedidiah, who flanked him—a habitual arrangement symbolic of accepted leadership, not unlike the position taken by the dominant male in a pack of wolves. The brothers wore identical black, high-crowned Stetsons with wide, flat brims, and greatcoats hanging loose and pulled back over the Colts at their waists. Dusty and trail-worn, they showed no sign of weariness, no diminished alertness. Quite the contrary. Their dark eyes burned with the fire of fierce determination, and vengeance was the spur that drove them.

The Blackthorns were not large men, each standing just

five-eight or under. Poured from the same mold, they were lean, lithe and whiplike in their movements. Quick as badgers, with tempers to match.

Jubal had been the youngest of the clan, a big, handsome man. But Jubal was dead, murdered from behind by a companion, a man he had trusted.

The feudal Blackthorns were reared in the remote backwoods of the Iron Mountains of Tennessee, living on squirrel and 'possum and bear, fighting and killing for food, fun and family.

Jacob had killed his first Klegg when he was a skinny, scraggly sprout of nine. John and Jedidiah were already blooded at the ages of ten and twelve. The storied Klegg-Blackthorn blood feud had been long resolved before baby Jubal could hoist a long rifle, the contest having run short on Kleggs. Pappy Blackthorn had been killed by a Klegg to start that mountain war. Mammy Emma, seeing her man's death avenged when the last Klegg was counted, had grieved herself to death. So, when Grandpap eventually passed on, the boys had moved West. They rambled for a spell, finally settling in West Texas, where they took to ranching.

The Blackthorn herd was an amazing, biologically puzzling, rapidly expanding congregation of cattle—all young stuff with muddled or obliterated brands. But no neighbor wondered at its makeup. No living neighbor. By armed might, the brothers forged an isolated, secure empire for themselves and their get, unquestioned and unchallenged. A family dynasty in the making.

Young Jubal had gone off to war, leaving his older brothers to build their empire. He found the civil struggle to his liking, but could not abide the regimentation, routine or submission to authority that the uniform required of him. So he fled the fields of battle, banding with others of his criminal bent to ravage the Western territories. Jubal Blackthorn never returned to West Texas.

His brothers had heard tell of Jubal from time to time, taking great pride in his nefarious enterprises, accomplishments and notoriety. Word of his death came as a bitter blow to the close-knit Blackthorn clan. They had hungered for revenge, but how could they extract blood justice from his slayers, an entire tribe of unknown savages?

Thus, they had welcomed the wicked truth that Caleb Free had carried to them. Brother Jubal, praise be, could and would be avenged. They rode now with hard and desperate comrades. They rode to bury Court Blaine.

The remaining three members of the evil entourage came behind the Blackthorns in staggered formation.

Caleb Free, astride a big black mule, slumped in the saddle. His deformed features were sweat-drenched and dirt-smeared, showing the bone-deep fatigue of an arduous trek. He, too, wanted to see Blaine get his due, but he was not so driven as the brothers. His whining complaints elicited nothing but a vicious threat from Jedidiah—

"Shut that puckered hole you call a mouth, 'fore I set fire to your face and beat out the flames with the butt of this here shotgun!"

—so he plodded now in silence.

Chinee, so christened by John Blackthorn, was a huge, glowering Oriental. Almond-shaped eyes, tilted like those of the Mongol barbarians of his ancestry, lacked the luster of intelligence, but held the predatory glint of a beast of prey. Tiny wisps of mustaches at the corners of his mouth accented his sinister intent. Chinee was a human instrument of death. Like a vicious trained watchdog he served one master—Peaceable John Blackthorn.

The last rider, as stoic as the Oriental and equally as deadly, was a Jicarilla Apache, Nachiteka. The Blackthorns called him "Tarantula." A Mexican sombrero concealed his face in dark shadow, though had he been hatless, one could have discerned nothing more from his expressionless features. Twin bandoleers crossed his chest over a homespun shirt. A brace of pistols rode his slender hips, butts facing forward. He wore spurs the size of supper plates.

Peaceable John held up a hand, halting the grim and grubby, grudge-ridden group on the lip of an outcropping. They considered the town of Raindance which lay lethargically sprawled on the floor of the valley below.

"Let's go among 'em. We've a polecat to skin."

The fate of his two friends preyed heavily on Jack's mind. After departing the Ute village, he crisscrossed the slopes, summits and valleys of the Sawatch, looking for a sign of what had become of Macklin and Hawkes, to no avail.

Dancer discovered the remains of Virgil Patch in the cave. The scavengers of the wild had scattered the bones while cleaning up, as best they could, the macabre mess left by man. Time, weather and the tracks of a procession of animals had effectively obliterated all indications of the drama that had occurred on the mountain and had erased the trails taken by the departing participants.

Jack pondered his next move while hunkered over a crackling fire, a steaming cup of coffee held to his lips. He alternately blew and sipped at the scalding brew.

He peered upward, past the gently swaying spires of the trees to the vivid blue of the summer sky. A light, south-west wind was slowly pulling a few thready clouds across his line of vision. From his lofty perch on the shelf, he regarded the land below him. There was a Sabbath grace to these mountains, with all of a dream's grandeur. It was a land that seemed outside of time. Squatting there, peering at the infinity extending out before him, the petty greeds and hatreds of mankind seemed inconsequential and far away.

Dancer forced his mind back to the situation at hand. Lord, he was tired of running into stone walls. Tired of questions that defied answers. He was ready for action.

His hand wandered aimlessly to his jaw and a two-inch shaggy growth of beard. His clothing was rumpled and crusted with dried blood, mud and the accumulated debris of his weeks away from the niceties of civilization. He doubted his sainted mother, rest her soul, would know him now. He glanced at the big bay grazing contentedly below him. A fine animal, but not the striking, memorable steed the appaloosa had been.

He stood up and lazily emptied the contents of the sooty coffeepot onto the embers of the campfire, spawning a hissing cloud of vapor. As he strapped on his gunbelt, his eyes visibly hardened. He was packing up. Jack Dancer was bound for a reckoning at Raindance.

"Oh, Court. It's beautiful."

Linda Macklin's blue eyes widened in wonder. She had never seen such a kaleidoscope of color. The meadow was choked with a wealth of wildflowers in a hundred hues—flaming red penstemon, crimson and golden columbine, trillium of white and delicate pinks. Yellow and white fairy bells pealed gently in the breeze. Asters and anemones, bellflowers and bluebells added their gaiety. Ox-eye daisies and Indian paint brush, even the lowly weeds joined the colorful chorus—the thistle with its pale purple crest, the pink of the showy milkweed. Marigolds and buttercups competed in brilliance with the late afternoon sun.

The mingled fragrances of the thousands of delicate blooms hung sweet and heavy in the air, enveloping the carriage in which Court and Linda sat side by side. She inhaled deeply, savoring the scented breeze. The gambler shifted uncomfortably. *Smells like a room full of perfumed trollops,* he mused.

Where in Hades were Stone Wolf and Worthy? Blaine wondered. He wanted this distasteful business done with. The gambler had taken great pains to ensure that no one had seen him leave town with Miss Macklin. He planned to be back in the saloon at his table when the evening's business was at its peak.

Linda sprang from the seat of the carriage and walked with a bouncy exuberance into the meadow to gather a bouquet. At that instant, two hooded riders leading a spare horse emerged from the trees on the slope opposite the creek. Intent upon her flower-gathering, she heard their approach before she saw them.

The masked riders moved between the young woman and the carriage, effectively blocking her retreat. Linda stood frozen in fear and shock, clutching poppies and evening primroses in her tiny fist.

Court Blaine rushed with long strides through the knee-high floral foliage to the scene, pretending outrage and anger. He challenged the mounted outlaws, demanding they leave at once.

"Wait, Court."

It was Linda. She recognized the prancing appaloosa that the nearest interloper was riding.

"Hello, Stone Wolf. And Worthy, is it? I don't doubt that you should want to hide your identities, considering the vile things you've done. What do you want here?"

The Indian muttered a disgusted oath. Worthy pulled the hood off his head, revealing an evil smile.

"Well, Blaine, no need to put on playin' the hero now. Missy, here, she knowed us right off." He chuckled, enjoying watching Blaine squirm.

"You, Court? You?" Linda's head whipped around toward her escort, a look of incredulity on her face.

"Why, yes'm," Worthy interjected, "Mr. Blaine, here, is the big boss man, the feller gives all the orders."

"Blast you, Worthy!" Blaine shouted, his eyes ablaze, "I told you to keep me clear of this!"

"No, sirree, boss man," Worthy said flatly. "We ain't

gonna be the only skunks in the henhouse if something goes sour. You'll be all the more careful of our well-bein' with your own neck in the noose."

Blaine ignored Linda's loathing look and strode angrily to the carriage, climbed aboard and took up the reins.

"Take her to the shack. I'll be in touch." Then, owing to a latent and contorted sense of chivalry, or perhaps merely from a gnawing fear of the consequences, the gambler added, "And keep your hands to yourself, both of you. If she's harmed, it'll be the costliest fun you're ever apt to have."

He turned the strutting black mare toward Raindance.

Chapter Twelve

Startled onlookers filtered from shops and stores onto the main street of Raindance as Rad Macklin rode into town. A small group of men, mouths agape and buzzing with surprised comments, followed the plodding horse of the "dead man" toward the sheriff's office.

Word of the rancher's resurrection spread quickly through the little town and, even as Macklin dismounted to tie his horse at the rail, Judge Handy and banker Wheeler led a cluster of leading citizens down the boardwalk toward Harley Brock's office door.

"I'm not all-fired sure that what you done ain't against some law or 'nother," Judge Handy told Macklin after the initial rash of questions and comments had been dispatched. "We dang near hanged a man for killing you."

"From what I hear, you didn't come all that close, Judge," Macklin said, putting his nose in the magistrate's face. "Seems to me you were mighty willing to put a noose around a stranger's neck without a shred of hard evidence, much less a body to prove a murder had taken place. And I'm not so sure *that* 'ain't against some law or 'nother,' as you so eloquently put it. Perhaps the governor would be interested in the quality of law being practiced in Raindance."

Handy blanched at the threat and his tone changed from one of indignation to that of whining supplication.

"Now, now, no need to make more of this than's been done already. No harm done, I reckon."

The eyes of the men in the small office and of those sticking their necks in the door all rested on Amos Handy. The judge tramped over and pushed the door closed. He turned red and asked, "Well, you going to tell us what this is all about?"

"That's what I'm here for."

Macklin proceeded to lay out the entire story for his small, rapt audience. He told them of the repeated attempts on his life, of meeting and becoming friends with his convicted "murderer," their decision to stage his funeral, the attempted killing of his foreman, Quint Hawkes, and of the murder of Jack Dancer during the attack on the ranch. He implicated his former hired hands—Stone Wolf, Patch and Worthy—then explained how Virgil Patch had met his end in the cave on the mountain.

"Where's Hawkes at?" the judge asked.

"Still in hiding," Macklin told him. "We decided that we mustn't both be exposed to these killers. If something happens to me, Hawkes will step in to right matters.

"I want you to swear out warrants for the arrest of the Indian, Stone Wolf, for murder and arson, and for Manfred Worthy on the charge of attempted murder. And on both for horse theft.

"Now gentlemen, I am most anxious to see my daughter. Do you know her whereabouts?"

"She's registered at the Pike House," Sheriff Brock volunteered.

Macklin hurried out the door, leaving the stunned town fathers busily muttering among themselves.

Linda was not in her room. Nor did the desk clerk know where she had gone, or when. Macklin roamed the streets, first checking the several eating establishments in town, then the dressmaker's, the doctor's office, and the general mercantile. Everywhere he wandered he dragged a tail of curious stares and bemused whispers. The townsmen hung back at a safe distance, unaccountably wary of a man they had thought to be dead.

No one Macklin asked seemed to have seen his daughter since the noon meal and the rancher grew increasingly concerned. Where might she have gone? Had she ridden to the ranch of a friend for a visit? He checked the livery. Linda's saddle horse was in its rented stall. Macklin walked quickly to the Golconda Saloon. Perhaps Court Blaine knew where she was.

"Macklin! Rad. I just heard the wonderful news."

Blaine jumped from his chair at the game table, swept a pile of chips off the felt into his ample palm and pocketed them, then rushed to greet the worried father entering the batwing doors of the saloon. He grasped the older man's hand in a warm greeting and slapped him on the shoulder, steering him toward the bar.

"This calls for a celebration. Mulroney," Blaine called out to the burly barkeep, "pour Mr. Macklin a drink."

"Court . . . have you seen Linda? Do you know where she might be?"

"Linda? Why, no, Rad. I haven't any idea where she is right now. I last saw her yesterday morning at breakfast. Did you check the hotel? She has a room there."

"I've been there . . . and everywhere else in town I could think of."

"Well, my friend, I wouldn't worry. She is no doubt having a chat with one of her lady friends here in town. Why not finish your drink, then check the hotel again to see if she has returned."

Macklin tossed off the whiskey and hurried back toward the Pike House. Blaine stood smiling at the doors the rancher left swinging in his wake.

"No, sir. I've still not seen your daughter," the emaciated little desk clerk told him. There was a sympathetic luster in the cataract-clouded eyes behind the thick, round lenses of his wire-rimmed glasses. "But someone laid this envelope on the counter while I was otherwise occupied. It is addressed to you, sir."

The harried rancher snatched the envelope from the clerk's extended hand. Hurriedly, he tore open the seal and read:

Macklin,

I have your daughter. If you want to see her alive again, follow these instructions exactly.

Meet me tomorrow at dawn, south of town on the Bent's Fort Trail where it crosses Blanca Creek. Come alone. Tell no one of this communication. Tell no one where you are going. Have the deed to the Flying M Ranch in your possession.

If you do as herein instructed, your daughter will not be harmed. She, and you, will be allowed to resume your lives unmolested. No variations. No tricks. I promise a most painful and disgraceful death for her, and for you, should you elect to disobey these directives.

The message was unsigned.

"Mr. Macklin? Is something wrong, sir?"

Stricken, Rad crumpled the offending note, stuffed it into

his coat pocket and turned away, stumbling dumbly out the door as the concerned clerk squinted after him.

Court Blaine idly riffled the cards on the table before him as Mulroney finished closing the saloon. He drew a long green cigar from the inside pocket of his coat, bit off the tip and spit it into the sawdust on the floor. He rolled the cigar in his pursed lips to wet the end, reversed it and lit it. He inhaled deeply, then, with a satisfied sigh, expelled the blue smoke in a hazy stream.

"Good take for a weeknight, Court," his bartender-partner observed as he stuffed the day's receipts into a cloth bag. "See you tomorrow."

Blaine nodded and watched the big Irishman go up the stairs, a sneer of disdain on his lips as he toyed absently with the waxed, twirled tip of his immaculate mustache. Court would be most happy to return full proprietorship of this dismal establishment to his dull cohort, once the gold was again securely in his possession. He picked up the lone lit lamp and climbed the stairs to his quarters.

Stifling a yawn, the gambler opened the door to his rooms. Three belted men stood in a row against the opposite wall.

"Who are you men? What are you doing in here?"

Peaceable John Blackthorn, a wad of tobacco the size of a goose egg bulging his cheek, stepped past Blaine and shut the door. As he turned back into the room he unleashed a vicious right that caught the gambler on the tip of the chin, sending him over a chair and into a bedside wash stand, tipping a pitcher of water to land upside down in his lap, upsetting the slop jar under the edge of the big four-poster.

Peaceable John pitched a palm-size length of leaded pipe into the air, caught it, then slipped it into the pocket of his coat.

"My little way of sayin' 'howdy,' " John said. "We be the Blackthorns . . . Jubal's kin."

The color drained from Blaine's face. Using the bed to steady himself, he clambered shakily to his feet.

"What do you want from me? You must know that Jubal Blackthorn has been dead for several years . . . massacred by Indians. I saw it happen. I was nearly killed as well."

The three brothers glowered knowingly, their eyes aglow with evil menace.

"Ain't the way we heard it. Heard tell you helped him along. We come nigh a thousand mile to right that wrong."

"No! Jubal was my friend. I was lucky to escape with my own life. Everyone else was killed."

"Not ever'body, slick talker. Caleb Free lives, and he bore witness to your deed. You're a dead man, Court Blaine."

"Not quite yet, yokel." A sleeve gun miraculously materialized in the gambler's hand. "Now back away, all of you. None of you need die, not just yet."

A cynical chuckle formed in Peaceable John's throat, emerging from his mouth as a full-blown guffaw.

"You reckon to kill us with that there two-shooter toy gun, gambler man? All three of us?"

The door burst open behind Blaine, spinning him around. Chinee, Tarantula and Caleb thundered into the room, their weapons coming to bear on the killer of Jubal Blackthorn. Resignedly, Court Blaine lowered his gun.

As a handsome and eligible young bachelor, Rad Macklin had been quite a ladies' man, sampling selectively from a delightful smorgasbord of female companions. Then he met Rebecca Pauley. Within weeks they were wed, and from that moment he became dedicated to the sanctity of that union. It had been the type of marriage that songs and sonnets praise, and Rad had been a happy man. Later, when Rebecca presented him with a darling baby daughter, his joy was multiplied. Then Rebecca had sickened and died, leaving Rad Macklin with a broken heart and a child to raise. He had met that challenge with an even greater outpouring of love and devotion, heaping upon Linda all the adoration he had held for his dear wife. Macklin doted on his daughter.

Now Linda was gone, snatched from the loving bosom of his protective charge, and, without her, Macklin was an empty man. He was obsessed with her safe return. He would stand against all challenges, meet any demand, make any sacrifice to secure his daughter's release.

After a sleepless night, Macklin had arrived at the specified rendezvous site an hour before dawn. He had waited impatiently until midmorning, checking and rechecking the rumpled ransom note a dozen times. Then he had ridden around the area for several hours, searching for the kidnapper.

What had gone wrong? Why hadn't the man showed? Macklin was frantic with worry for his daughter. He returned to the original location to wait some more.

Finally, as dusk darkened into night, Rad reluctantly turned his horse toward Raindance. There was no recourse except to return to the hotel. Perhaps another message awaited him. He slumped wearily in the saddle, forcing back the tears.

The brim of the lone horseman's black hat was pulled low over his eyes against the stabbing glare of the silver shafts of sunrise that topped the timbered summits east of Raindance. The glint of sunlight shone off the polished stocks of rifle and shotgun in their scabbards on opposite sides of the saddle. His hand rested on his right thigh, near the walnut grip of the Colt .44 in the holster on his hip. Jack Dancer cleared the outskirts of town and headed down the center of a slowly wakening back street.

Under the stubble, the steel set of the rider's jaw signaled his no-nonsense mood and serious intent. He had come to

Raindance for a resolution to the trouble; and he was primed for a fight.

A yowling pack of barefoot youngsters bounded into the street, chunking pine cones at one another, giving off a shrill chorus of menacing shouts and raucous laughter that startled the bay. The glowering countenance of the horseman brought them to a skidding halt and hushed them. The racket started up again as he rounded the corner onto the main street, causing Dancer to grin despite his grave mission.

A cock crowed across town and a dog yelped somewhere beyond the clapboard fronts as he passed the Golconda Saloon. He cast a withering glance toward the batwing doors where his involvement in the present sticky state of affairs had begun, then pushed the blood bay on past the rumps of two horses at the rail—a line-back dun, lazily swishing its tail, and a chestnut, sides quivering to shake off the flies.

Dancer pulled up in front of the sheriff's office, dismounted, stepped onto the boardwalk and kicked in the scabbed gray door.

Sheriff Harley Brock lay on his cot in a puddle of his own vomit. The lawman looked as if he had been dragged face down through the streets of Raindance. His face was a puffy, pulpy mess. He had a broken nose and a badly split, swollen lip. His right eye had swelled shut, the left was blood-red and both sockets were as black as a banker's heart. His cheeks and forehead were covered with freshly scabbed cuts and abrasions. The big man's gun hand was swathed in bandages, the right arm in a sling. In his meaty left fist he clutched a whiskey bottle by the neck, with scant remains in the bottom. The sheriff of Raindance was tongue-chewing, babbling drunk.

"What in the everlovin' blue-eyed world got hold of you, Harley?"

Tears welled up in the beefy lawman's lone open eye as he attempted to focus it on the manhunter. He grimaced as he struggled to form his outsized upper lip around the words.

"Bwackfoans. Bwack . . . fowens. Dag bwast it!"

"All right, big fella. You lay back and relax a spell. I'll brew us up a washtub or so of coffee, then we'll try again later."

Dancer reached to take the bottle from Brock's hand as the battered behemoth belched juicily and fell face forward on the cot, out stone cold.

Three hours and a gallon of black coffee later, Dancer was able to piece together what had occurred from the laborious and convoluted blatherings of a sickened and abashed Harley Brock.

A pack of gun-toting ruffians, six men in all, had effectively taken over the town of Raindance, terrifying the good citizens into submission, commandeering whatever struck their fancies—whiskey, food, working girls, money, guns or goods. The group was led by three brothers named Blackthorn, but the beating the sheriff had received had been administered by a huge Oriental man.

As the story of the siege unfolded, Dancer felt a thrilling elation. A fight was in the offing. Here was something tangible against which he could strike.

"Dancer, Macklin showed up a couple days ago, alive and kickin'. Means you can't very well've killed him, I reckon. I, for one, want to say how sorry I am for all the ruckus."

"Macklin? Where is he?"

"The Pike House, last I heard."

Dancer wheeled around and started out the door, pausing with the knob in his hand as the sheriff continued.

"I'm beholden for what you done, Dancer. You best tread light around town . . . shy clear of the Blackthorns. That's a bad bunch."

"They haven't seen *bad* yet, Harley."

Her dress had been torn away when she struggled to break free of her captors. She was wearing only undergarments and high-heeled boots of soft tanned leather. Her long blond hair hung in matted ropes around her white shoulders. Ugly welts and bruises covered her face in mute testimony to the brutal treatment of her captivity. Her grimy cheeks were streaked by tears, long since shed and expended.

Nothing in Linda Macklin's life experience had in any way prepared her for the inhumane, heinous and horrifying assaults upon mind and body that had been inflicted upon her in this hidden mountain cabin. She knew full well that, considering the treatment she had received from her captors, she must eventually be killed, forever silenced. She resigned herself to that gruesome fact—even welcomed the thought of it. The only hope she still harbored was that in some way she might be able to strike back, to inflict some measure of revenge upon the beasts that had so foully used her.

Linda's hands were bound securely behind her back, the rawhide thongs cutting into the flesh at her wrists. Her legs had been left free, but she was hobbled like a horse, allowing her a limited mobility for the convenience of her tormentors. She was alone in the cabin now, but there was no hope of escape. The place was a fortress, built to withstand attack from Indians or posses. The heavy door and shutters were securely barred from outside.

So she sat, numbed beyond pain and anguish, drained even of terror. Linda awaited whatever fate was in store, wanting only to kill and to die.

A fumbling at the barred door announced the return of one of the kidnappers. Linda leaned to a bunk near her and grabbed the edge of a tattered blanket with her teeth, pulling it as best she could to cover her legs and lower body. Then she scooted backward across the splintered, rough plank floor into a corner where she crouched, making herself as small as she could. The door was thrust open, the accompanying gust stirring into action a herd of dust balls the size of tumbleweeds across the unswept floor. Manfred Worthy tromped in. He was drunk, and lusty as a goat.

"Well now, how's my little playmate? I'm back. Bet you missed your new best friend, huh missy?"

He grinned lecherously at the pathetic, cringing figure in the corner, then advanced, stumbling toward her.

A few scattered patrons sat close-mouthed, grim-faced and jittery in the Golconda, afraid to stay, terrified of leaving, wincing at the tortured screams of agony that emanated with regularity from the gambler's quarters on the floor above. As nerve-wrenching as the screaming were the intervals between, filled with low moans of torment and pain. One could only speculate and fantasize at the manner of gruesome punishment being exacted upon the poor wretch in the rooms overhead.

The Blackthorn brothers seemed oblivious to the tension in the air and the macabre activity upstairs. They sat at separate strategic stations in the saloon, with long-barreled, staghorn-handled sixguns on the table tops before them. They drank from the necks of complimentary whiskey bottles, holding blanched and quivering saloon girls on their laps.

Mulroney sagged behind the bar, like a candle placed near a potbellied stove. The big Irishman's face was devoid of color, his brow beaded with nervous sweat. His hooded, yellow eyes darted from one outlaw brother to another, alert to the occasion when one might want for fresh whiskey or a fresh girl. The barkeep had witnessed the efficient and brutal bludgeoning of the sheriff by their Oriental henchman and was determined to anticipate the Blackthorns' every whim, that he might escape a similar fate.

Jacob Blackthorn rose suddenly from his seat near the rear entrance, pitching the girl that had been perched on his legs roughly to the sawdust-covered floor. With a roar he shouted, "More whiskey! And find me a woman can keep her balance! This'n keeps fallin' off a man's lap."

He burst forth in guttural laughter at his self-perceived cleverness. As the discarded hostess vanished, the barkeep was dragging a fresh but reluctant replacement toward him by the arm. And so progressed the evening.

Overhead, Chinee and Tarantula were taking a respite from their joint venture of torture. The Oriental lay asleep on the bed. The Apache reclined on the floor, his eyes narrowed slits in his tobacco-colored features. Court Blaine slumped, bare-chested, bound to a chair. The moribund gambler's head drooped limply against his chest. A raw, blood-caked patch at the crown of his skull spoke of the Indian's skill with a scalping knife, repayment for what Blaine had done to the youngest Blackthorn. His arms, tied to his sides and around the back of the chair, hung limp. The once nimble fingers of both hands had been broken by the Mongol, ensuring that the card sharp would never deal another ace from the bottom of the deck. Blaine's slack frame was settled into a pool of his own filth.

The once handsome and confident Blaine bore scant resemblance to the swaggering man who had ordered Linda Macklin kidnapped. The vicious and coldly calculated butchery inflicted upon him by his captors had eaten away at the very soul of the man. The jaunty mustache on his lip now hung limp and drenched in sweat-diluted blood, framing his down-turned mouth and transforming his face into a darkly comical mask of tragedy. His eyes bulged in their sockets from straining against the painful insults his body had been forced to endure. His face was a pulpy mass of bruises and abrasions. Only the man's own greed-hardened will had stayed his spirit from crossing the thread-thin line that separated the spark of life from the dark, quiet abyss of death.

The soles of Blaine's swollen feet were blistered and weeping from the injury of dozens of cruel burns. Although unconscious, Blaine wailed weakly, the sound of a soul in torment.

Earlier, the brothers had argued vehemently among themselves over the fate of their sibling's killer. Jedidiah and Jacob had insisted upon killing him outright. Peaceable John had voted for a slower, more creative death. The conflict was resolved when Caleb Free remembered the gold—the fabulously rich, unrecovered prize of Jubal Blackthorn's final foray. It was evident to the group that Court Blaine must have escaped with the gold, and that he had it cached somewhere. They were determined to have that information, so had commissioned Chinee and Tarantula to extract it from their brother's former lieutenant. The means to that end had been left in their capable hands, for John Blackthorn knew that no more methodical or inventive practitioners existed than the pair on his payroll.

Blaine had shown more grit than expected, suffering through hour after hour of grueling and excruciating punishment, martyring himself, defiantly refusing to divulge his secret.

"I got to grant you," Peaceable John commented in grudging admiration, "the man's got *cajones*."

A satanic light fired the Indian's eyes. An uncharacteristic smile crossed his lips.

"Not for long," he said.

Chapter Thirteen

As Dancer and Macklin rode into the makeshift camp of Quint Hawkes, the lanky Flying M foreman was sitting on the plush needle carpet of the forest floor in the shade of an ill-constructed lean-to. His long legs were stretched out in front of him and he was whittling a stick into a toothpick. As he recognized the long rider on the blood bay, his mouth gaped and he sprang to his feet, solidly rapping his head on the unforgiving roof of the shelter. "Ouch," he said.

"Just as nimble as ever, I see," Dancer quipped. "Good to see you, Hawkes."

The cowboy thrust out his right hand in greeting as he gently caressed his new knot with the other hand.

"Tarnation. I never seen the like of folks poppin' back from the dead as they do in these parts. Howdy, Dancer. How come you ain't buried? What happened?"

"Later," interrupted a grim-faced Macklin as he dismounted, "we've got problems to talk about." The three men sat cross-legged and facing each other in a tight circle on the ground. Now angry, now frightened, the beleaguered rancher filled his foreman in on Linda's disappearance, showed

127

him the ransom note and told him of his fruitless vigil at Blanca Creek at which the kidnapper failed to show.

"You're plumb lucky he didn't show up, Rad, for whatever reason," said Dancer. "You'd be dead meat for sure. Once he makes himself known to you, he has to kill you to protect himself."

"I don't care about me. We've got to help Linda. I want my daughter free of that monster."

"*Those* monsters. He won't be working alone, my friend," Jack said. "Just simmer down. We'll find her . . . if she's still alive."

"Goldern you, Dancer! You got no call to say that."

"It's an ugly possibility we've got to consider. They can no more afford for Linda to be free to name them than they can allow you to stay alive. Either way would mean the noose for them, and they will be thinking of just that.

"But I figure they'll keep her alive, at least until they've gotten what they're after . . . the Flying M. Seems to have been the ranch all along, or more likely something hidden on the ranch.

"And the drastic measures they've taken can spell only one thing. Money. Lots of money."

"Consarn it, Jack, I don't know anything about any money."

"Of course you don't, but whoever has your daughter knows, or thinks he does.

"That can wait, though. The first order of business is to get Linda free of the kidnappers. We need to analyze this thing and make plans. Going off half-cocked in every direction will only get her killed. Us too, likely.

"What about this bunch in town now? The Blackthorns. Could they be mixed up in this?" asked Jack.

"I don't see how," Macklin said, shrugging. "I never even heard of them until they hit town two days ago."

"Blackthorn, you say?" Quint asked. "Wasn't there a

Blackthorn gang of renegades runnin' the territories a few years back? Robbery? Murder?"

Dancer slapped his forehead with the butt of his palm.

"Of course! The Jubal Blackthorn gang. This bunch must be Jubal's kin. Can't imagine why I didn't connect it before now.

"The story is the gang waylaid a rich shipment of gold up around Climax. Killed the guards and outriders and got away with four wagons of high-grade ore.

"Then they got hit by a band of renegade Utes. Wiped them out, all of them, or so it was thought. But no trace of the gold was ever found. Just empty wagons and outlaws' bones. Folks figured the Indians made off with the gold, but thinking on it now, that makes no sense. They couldn't sell it . . . or haul it away for that matter, without the wagons.

"No, I'll bet someone was left alive of that outlaw bunch, or someone came across the scene and made off with the gold."

"I still don't see what that has to do with me or with Linda being kidnapped," Macklin said.

"Everything, man. The gold is buried somewhere on the Flying M."

Macklin and Hawkes looked at each other in astonished realization as the evident truth of Dancer's supposition struck home.

"Here's what we'll do. Hawkes, you go back to the ranch and keep watch. Stay well back and well hidden. Pick a spot from where you can see as much of the ranch as possible. If I'm right, sooner or later somebody is going to come for that gold. My guess is it won't be long. This thing is coming to a head.

"Rad, you and I will start at Blanca Creek . . . try to pick up some sort of trail or sign. We'll find Linda, or die trying."

"Hold on, Dancer," Hawkes objected, "I want in on this action. I don't give two hoots and a holler about any gold, and I ain't one for sittin' and waitin'. I want to go with you to get Linda loose, and I want a piece of the mangy skunks that took her."

"I know how you feel, Quint, but it's all-important that we cover every possibility. If Rad and I don't find her, or if we get shot up trying to get her away, whoever comes for that gold could be the only lead to Linda's whereabouts. You keep watch like I said. Don't brace them, just keep them in sight. When we finish, or if we fail, we'll come back to get you before any showdown. We'll need you. You'll see plenty of action, I promise you.

"Now let's get going."

Dancer and Macklin stayed in camp just long enough to finish off a pot of coffee, then rode away, leaving the grumbling cowboy to his assigned duty.

By the time the seekers reached the site of the earlier rendezvous at Blanca Creek it was full dark, so they made a small fire for coffee and laid out their bedrolls, forced to wait for daylight to begin their search.

"If we don't find any kind of trail tomorrow, Macklin, I'm going back into Raindance. That's where the answer lies."

"The Blackthorns? You going to face them?"

"I'll most likely be forced to it. But I believe Court Blaine is the key to this. He is our man. He is the one that has wanted the ranch all along . . . and he's no rancher by a long sight."

"If that's true I'll kill the sonofagun with my own bare hands!"

"Sorry, partner. That's one pleasure I'm saving for myself."

"Not a chance. She's my *daughter*."

"But, if we all come out of this in one piece, I'm asking her to be *my wife*."

* * *

First light was but a paling of the pewter clouds that hung low and heavy overhead, obscuring white-hooded peaks that dispatched an icy, carnivorous wind in sweeping, gusting blasts along the banks of the creek and into camp, negating any cheering benefit of the cookfire in the clearing. Dancer nudged the rancher from the warmth of his bedroll, sticking a tin plate of beans and curled bacon under his nose. The two men ate in silence, split a pot of coffee and each lit a smoke. Swinging the pot to scatter the grounds, Dancer walked to the clear, rushing creek for fresh water as Macklin rolled and packed his bedding behind his saddle. Only as the second pot of black, heart-starting liquid began to boil did either man speak.

"So where do we start?" Macklin asked.

Dancer turned his head slowly, taking in the surrounding terrain.

"They will have her well off the trail where no one's apt to stumble across them, and in an area with good cover. I'm sure we can rule out any known ranches or homesteads. They wouldn't chance hangman's hemp on being found out by some drifter riding the grub line.

"My guess is they're holed up somewhere near here in high-er country. A proven hideout they've used before, perhaps.

"You go back up the trail a few miles and sweep both sides. Look for a spot where the ground might be chewed up from horses milling about, for wagon tracks, cigarette butts . . . anything unusual that indicates someone waiting or that a confrontation has taken place. Work your way up on this side," Dancer said with a sweep of his arm, "then come back on the other a couple miles past camp, then back to this spot on this side again. Take your time so you don't miss something. Remember though, you were all over while you were waiting to make contact with the kidnapper. Don't wind up tracking yourself."

"I know my own horse's prints," snapped Macklin. "What about you? What are you going to do?"

"I'll round that meadow of flowers across the creek, then keep widening my circle, see if I can spot any tracks where they might have come down out of the trees.

"If one of us finds something we'll fire off a shot."

At the belligerent, grumbling challenge of thunder, Jack raised a seasoned eye to an angry, leaden sky.

"It's going to bust loose in a couple of hours. Let's hope we find some sign before we're rained out."

They rose simultaneously. Macklin stuck a boot in the stirrup and swung a leg over. He looked down with hollowed, dark-circled eyes at Jack Dancer to see a man as hardrock tough as the mountains he rode, as game as a fighting cock, pouring the last of the coffee on the coals.

"Jack. Thank you. Whether we are successful in this or not, I'm ever in your debt. And I'd be mighty proud to count you as my son-in-law."

Dancer grinned as he settled in the saddle.

"I reckon we'll both have to leave that up to Linda, won't we?"

Meanwhile, not five miles away at the hideaway shack, its shingled sides shaggy with ivy, Worthy and Stone Wolf sat hunched over a shared bottle of sour mash whiskey, concernedly discussing their situation.

"Should have heard from Blaine before now." Stone Wolf growled out his complaint, visibly uneasy. "You think maybe he got what he wanted, then broke camp? You think he's left us behind to be caught with this girl?"

"It'd be the sort of nasty thing that back-bitin' weasel would stoop to, sure enough," answered Worthy. "Fact is, it'd be a thing I'd stoop to my own self, come to think on it. What do you figger we'd ought to do?"

"I will go, ride to town. See what is going on. You stay with the girl."

"Oh, yeah? And just what's to stop you from ridin' off and

leavin' me stuck with the whole blasted caboodle of wormy meat?"

"Nothing. Nothing to stop me from killing you now, and the girl, if I want. Nothing to stop me from doing what I please . . . but I will do as I say. It means much money.

"If I am not back in two days, you will know that all is not as we planned. Kill the girl and go. You agree?"

"I agree."

The Comanche gathered his gear, threw a bait of grub into an empty salt sack and left the cabin.

Worthy slumped morosely in his chair, scratching his beard. He took a long pull from the neck of the whiskey bottle, slamming it down on the scarred table before him. He toyed absently with the deep-cut indentations of crudely fashioned letters, words and symbols that disfigured the abused table top, carved by the hand of some holed-up, bored marauder from years past. He glanced over at the girl on the bunk, sitting in a fetal position with her back leaned against the plank wall of the shack. Her eyes stared blankly into space. Her face had the dead beauty of marble. Her features hung slack. Where the blanket across her shoulders gapped open in front, a lacy garment peeked through, a mocking contrast to her surroundings and situation.

"You ain't too talky, are you wench? . . . I like that in a woman."

"You'll kill me anyway."

"You're takin' it all wrong, y'know. Since the boss says to leave you be, just look at this as a religious ceremony, miss. We're fixin' to sacrifice a virgin."

Worthy broke out in carnal laughter, watching the captive girl for a reaction. Her expression remained unchanged. He looked around the cabin as if searching for something and, finding nothing, finally settled his gaze back upon the forlorn figure on the cot.

Worthy stood clumsily, the whiskey humming in his veins, upsetting his chair. It fell backward to the floor with a clatter.

Dancer peered at the barely visible, days-old tracks in the soft earth at the edge of the timber. He was raising his pistol in the air to fire a signal when he heard the report of Macklin's rifle from across the meadow. Jack holstered the .44, then turned the bay's nose in the direction of the shot. He rode slowly along the shore of the blossoming sea of wildflowers, his eyes trained to the ground. He pulled up on the reins and climbed from the saddle, knelt on one knee and stared at the patch of dirt in front of him. Having catalogued in his mind what he had observed, he swung back into the saddle and led off at a canter toward Rad Macklin, his horse cutting a wake knee-deep through the brilliant waves of blooming foliage.

The rancher stood reins in hand, waiting for Jack to approach. A flush of excitement was on his face.

"Jack boy, I think I've found something," he said elatedly, casting a shaky forefinger earthward.

Dancer pulled up and dismounted, leaving the reins of the bay to hang free. He walked over and hunkered down above the evidence that Macklin indicated.

"See . . . wagon tracks."

Dancer shook his head.

"Carriage. Too narrow for a wagon. Sat here hitched for quite a spell. See how the wheels rolled back and forth when the horse moved?"

Dancer let his eyes roam the ground.

"See these small bootprints, Rad? They're Linda's. She lit down out of the buggy and walked into the meadow.

Dancer's steady gaze studied every pebble, leaf and grain. He pointed again.

"These tracks belong to a man. He was hurrying, same direction as Linda."

Jack paused and frowned. "And here . . . the man came back, alone.

"This was a big man, Macklin, like Court Blaine. And Blaine owns a carriage."

Macklin colored.

"We going after him?"

"Not just yet. I found something, too, over yonder. I was fixing to fire off a round when I heard your signal."

They rode together across the field until Dancer held up a hand, calling a halt.

"They came out of the timber about a hundred yards off that way," he said gesturing. "Two mounted men leading a riderless horse.

"These are the tracks of the same horses heading back, all ridden this time. The one in the middle is carrying someone small . . . Linda. And Rad," Dancer said pointing, "this is a print left by *my appaloosa*.

"Now we know who we're after. Stone Wolf and Worthy are holding your daughter, Court Blaine is calling the shots."

Dancer began checking the loads in his guns. Macklin followed suit. As they climbed atop their horses, raindrops as big as dollars began to plop around them. By the time they hit the timber they were riding in a torrential downpour.

For an hour the pair slogged through the deluge with the rain resounding off their ankle-length slickers like the constant fire of a hundred rifles. It became impossible to follow any tracks that might have existed in the semi-darkness of the forest, but Dancer led on, riding his mind down the possible trails their quarry might have taken. The men rode in silent determination, for the roar of the storm swallowed all attempts at shouted conversation. Finally Jack signaled his partner toward the shelter of an overhang.

Once under the protective shelf, away from nature's ill-timed and pitiless pelting, the drenched searchers stepped down from their wet saddles to shake the water from the wide brims of their Texas hats and peel off their raincoats. Both mounts stood quivering with the dampness, the cold and the fear of nature's fury, their coats glistening black with rain. Dancer began to rub down the bay with the heel of his hand, sending sheets of water ahead of each thrust. Exhausted, Macklin slid down the stone back wall of the shelter to a squatting position, resting his forehead on his arms.

As they rested, smoking, Dancer turned to Macklin, screaming to be heard over the continued deafening barrage of the downpour.

"We've had it, Rad! This rain would wash out any trail not made of cobblestone. You rest up . . . I'm going into Raindance!"

"No . . . not without me, you ain't!" Macklin roared back.

"There'll more than likely be gunplay!" Dancer shouted. "That's work I'm cut out for. Let me handle it. I don't want to have to tell Linda, when we find her, that I got her daddy killed!"

"I can back you, boy. I've got to go. You got no right to ask me not to!"

Dancer read the despair in the harried father's expression and placed an understanding hand on his damp shoulder.

"It's your neck! I reckon we'll handle it together. Let's mount up!"

Chapter Fourteen

P eaceable John Blackthorn, his brother Jedidiah and Caleb Free had departed Raindance at dawn, the same time that Dancer and Macklin had been breakfasting on Blanca Creek. The brothers were perched on the spring seat of a large wagon pulled by a four-horse team. Their chestnut saddle horses trailed behind, reins tied to the gate. Caleb Free followed at the reins of a plodding team pulling a second, smaller wagon. The beds of both vehicles were empty of cargo, save a scattered assortment of shovels, picks, sledges, ropes, buckets and a wooden box filled with food and camp gear, sufficient supplies for the trio for three days.

The imminent threat of lost manhood had persuaded the long-suffering Blaine to reveal the location of his golden treasure. The excavation party had set out straightaway. John instructed Jacob Blackthorn to remain at the saloon with Chinee and the Tarantula to keep the cowed populace of Raindance under wraps and to keep Court Blaine alive until the information forced from him could be verified. As the goldseekers neared the Flying M, the bulging black bellies of fire-charged clouds ruptured as if gutted by some great, unseen blade. They were at once inundated by a driving,

137

pounding rain. Slapping the teams into a profanity-inspired run, they bounced and careened crazily along the rutted road, desperately seeking shelter to wait out the storm. The wagons sped sliding into the ranchyard past the charred skeletal remains of both house and bunkhouse to the three-sided shed at the rear of the big corral. The lumbering wagons skidded to a sloshing halt under the only structure remaining on the Flying M that offered shelter from the merciless storm.

Quint Hawkes, posted in a thick stand of pale-trunked aspen atop a high bluff overlooking the ranchyard, missed the outlaws' coming as he, himself, scurried to escape the drenching onslaught from the heavens.

The rain had all but ended by the time Macklin and Dancer rode in, and an impatient sun was trying to burn a path through the thinning clouds. The storm had made a wallow of the main street. The hooves of their bedraggled horses made obscene sucking noises in the mud with each laboring step. The riders halted in front of Pike House, retrieved soaked bedrolls from behind their saddles, hitched the animals to the rail and entered the lobby of the hotel, leaving mounds of mud behind each step. They went directly to Macklin's room to rest, dry out and to discuss their next move.

Allowing his slicker to slip to the floor, Jack peeled off his shirt with a slurping sound, exposing a lean and hard, oft-scarred torso. Steel cords of muscle rippled under his skin as he moved. A dark tan vee at his neck and "sleeves" halfway up his forearms contrasted comically with the stark white pallor of his body. He carried the dripping shirt to a night stand and twisted it tightly, wringing water into a porcelain basin.

Macklin peeled off his wet clothes, down to faded red longjohns, depositing his outerwear in a heap at the foot of the spindle bed. He flopped wearily onto an acre of feather mattress, asleep almost instantly.

Dancer hung the damp shirt on a chair back, repeated the wringing exercise with his stockings and denim pants, then joined the rancher on the bed. Soon his gentle snore underscored Macklin's more robust snorting.

It was dark and moonless outside the second-story window when Dancer, the first to stir, opened his eyes. He groped in the blackness for his shirt and pulled a small oilskin-wrapped package from the chest pocket, withdrawing a sulfur match. He brought the match to life against the bedpost, squinting at the sudden glare, then reached for a coal oil lamp on the bureau. Lifting the chimney he lit the wick and set the lamp back on the bureau top. Jack dressed in still-damp clothes, then sat on the edge of the bed to roll a smoke. He lit the cigarette at the chimney of the lamp and inhaled deeply with satisfaction.

Macklin was mumbling in his sleep, of his little girl Linda, of ranchhouse fires and brown-skinned snipers and of empty graves. Dancer reached to shake him gently awake.

"Time to go?" Rad questioned sleepily, grinding the heels of his hands in his eyes.

"Get dressed. We'll go get some supper and puzzle out how best to go about this."

There were no dining facilities at the small hotel so, after stabling the horses at the livery, the rancher and the hunter of men waded ankle-deep in muddy ooze to Maude's Home Cooking—Eats and Bakery, two doors east of the Golconda Saloon. They seated themselves at one of four small round tables spread with red-checkered oil cloths situated against the rear wall of a cramped dining area. By the time they had settled into their chairs, Maude was at Macklin's elbow placing heavy crockery mugs in front of them. She filled the mugs with steaming coffee from an enameled pot and handed each man a hand-written bill of fare.

"Evenin' gents," Maude greeted them brightly.

She was a buxom woman of above average height, stockily built, with a face permanently reddened from years spent with her nose in a hot oven. She looked German, with straight blond hair pulled back severely into a bulky bun on the back of her neck. Stray wisps hung from either side of her wide, flat brow, framing her green eyes like parentheses. She wore no face paint and needed none. The woman sported an infectious smile that drew like expressions from the two men.

"What might I serve you gents this evening?"

"Are the Blackthorns still in town? Still got the place buffaloed?"

The smile faded from the woman's ruddy face at Jack's question and she shifted uncomfortably.

"Mister, I serve up two things here . . . the best darn food this side of the Divide and coffee strong enough to make a brave man cry. Other than that I tend my own knittin'. I want no trouble with anyone."

"Fair enough . . . Maude, is it?"

"It is. What'll you have?"

"I'll try the pot roast and gravy. How about you, Rad?"

"Same."

Maude topped off their coffee mugs and disappeared into the kitchen.

Both men ate ravenously from generous servings, Dancer opting for seconds on biscuits and gravy.

"Rad, I'll go in first," Dancer told him, sopping up the last of the rich, brown gravy with a crust of biscuit, "order a drink at the bar, makin' out like I'm just passing through. You come in through the rear. Don't fire or make any kind of fuss unless it's to back my play. I'd as soon this not come to gunplay, though I doubt it can be avoided.

"We'll have to play it as it falls, not knowing the situation inside. Just follow my lead and we'll make out fine.

"We've got to get Blaine alone to find out where he's holding Linda. You ready?"

"Ready."

"Good luck, partner."

They scooted their chairs noisily away from the table. Dancer flipped a dollar onto the checkered cloth, the heavy clunk bringing Maude scooting around the corner. She looked at both men with concern, as if she somehow knew what they were about.

"Take care."

"Thanks," said Jack, saluting with the tip of his finger against the brim of his black hat.

"I'll be making mince meat pie tomorrow," she shouted after them from the door as they walked solemnly and purposefully toward the saloon.

After Macklin rounded the corner of the building, headed for the back door of the Golconda, Dancer paused in front of the swinging doors and fingered his gun up and down in its holster to make sure it slid easily. He bunched his shoulders, tipped his hat further down over his eyes and stepped inside. He surveyed the layout in an instant.

A few patrons were bunched in twos and threes at the bar and at scattered tables around the interior. None appeared to be armed.

A small, dark man, his wide-brim hat perched cockily on the back of his head, sat at a table facing the entrance with a bottle of whiskey before him, no glass. A gaudily and scantily attired woman was perched on his lap. The excessive lip rouge and heavily applied blush on her cheeks furnished the only color in the soiled dove's frightened face.

Just inside the batwing doors to the manhunter's right lurked a huge Oriental man, leaning against the front wall. Flapped lids gave his hard, narrow eyes a tilted appearance.

Expressionless features offered no hint of human feeling. The man was built like a redwood. He was bare from the waist up except for an intricately embroidered vest of shiny fabric. Cords of muscle, thick as ferry ropes, writhed beneath his tawny hide like snakes in a pit. A keen blade, thirty inches long and slightly curved, was held at his thick waist in a black cloth sash. Involuntarily, Dancer shuddered.

Jack stepped to the bar to place a muddied boot on the foot rail.

"Hey, you."

It was the small man at the table speaking. Dancer ignored him.

"You that just sauntered in the door . . . big man," Jacob said with added force, "I'm talking to you."

Dancer turned slowly and fixed the speaker with a stare cold enough to ice down beer kegs.

"Talking to me, shortcakes?"

Jacob Blackthorn flushed and sputtered.

"This here's a Blackthorn town. No firearms allowed. I'll bother you for your iron. You get it back when you ride out."

"I reckon not."

Instantly angered at the newcomer's defiance, the diminutive outlaw whipped a glance toward the Oriental and nodded toward the insolent stranger in black.

"Chinee . . ."

The lumbering henchman bored in with a feral growl, one big hand on the hilt of the sword in his sash.

"Call off your overgrown Pekinese," Dancer warned.

The outlaw grinned as he said it. "Kill him, Chinee."

A savage smile lit the face of the dusky-skinned assassin as he lurched toward his target, drawing and wielding the blade in one slashing blur of motion.

Dancer reacted instantly, ducking beneath the mighty swipe, losing his hat to the sweeping sword. He drove a knee to the groin of his outsized attacker, bending him double and eliciting a surprised howl of agony. Jack followed with a slashing uppercut to the flat, broad nose, sending his formidable foe reeling backward in a spray of blood, yowling in pain and fury. The sword dropped from Chinee's hand and buried itself in the sawdust on the floor. Dancer bored in with a flurry of right and left crosses to the head and body, so swift and punishing that his target was helpless to retaliate.

The Oriental shuffled back and away, swinging his head and slavering like some bewildered beast, beads of sweat popping forth on his furrowed forehead. He bent low and growled—a primitive, guttural cry of anguished rage. Hoisting a huge knotty fist, he charged, astoundingly quick and nimble for so large a man.

Chinee dove at the smaller man, grabbed him around the legs and jerked them from under him. As he fell, Dancer stabbed for his opponent's eyes with a thumb. Chinee jerked his head away and Dancer jammed the hard heel of his hand under the chin, pushed him back and broke his crushing grip. An overhand right aimed for the brute's nose landed low on his throat. The Oriental fell back, choking and gasping for breath as Dancer rolled free, kicking him behind the knees and sending him crashing to the saloon floor. Jack came to his feet and backed away, struggling to clear his head and catch his breath.

Chinee emerged from the sawdust on the floor to his knees like a storm cloud building, and as he did his hand found the haft of his errant sword. He came off the floor with a barbarian scream, slashing the air with mighty strokes of the sinister blade. He advanced toward Dancer, blood lust in his eyes. He increased speed toward the object of his fury with the scream in his throat building to a deafening crescendo.

"Stop!" yelled Dancer, then his gun was in his hand. The .44 bucked once, twice.

Dancer stepped aside as the Oriental plunged through the

bar like a wounded buffalo through a rail fence and took the splintered end of the counter to the floor with a resounding crash. There the fury ended. Chinee's huge body lay still.

"Lordamighty!" Blackthorn was stunned and mesmerized by the violent confrontation he had witnessed.

"Jack, boy, look out!"

Dancer spun at Macklin's shouted warning, diving head-first under the nearest table. A bullet plowed into the bar where he had been standing an instant before, erupting a cloud of splinters. The Tarantula stood crouched on the stairway, a plume of smoke rising from the barrel of a Winchester in his hand. Again the Apache raised the rifle, drawing a fresh bead on Dancer, who was now struggling to regain his feet. Macklin fired at the Indian and missed. The Tarantula swept his aim swiftly toward the rancher, firing at Macklin as Dancer brought his own gun into play. Two shots sounded. The Tarantula's bullet dropped Macklin like a blow from a sledgehammer, blood gushing from a wound to the head. The shot from Dancer's Colt caught the Indian below the waist, sitting him down on the bottom stair with a rude jolt.

All this while, Jacob Blackthorn had been sitting at his table, a spectator to the carnage around him. Now he rose slowly, sliding back his chair with deliberation. He stepped toward Dancer, flexing his fingers, his hand poised above the staghorn butt of his Colt revolver.

"You want some of me, little man?" Blood running hot, Dancer barked his challenge

"You done made your last mistake, hero. I ain't never seen a gunhand faster'n me."

"In that case," Dancer replied with a wry smile, "you are in for a rare and unforgettable treat."

Blackthorn went for his gun, his hand a blur. He was fast.

Chapter Fifteen

J acob Blackthorn lay face down in the sawdust on the floor of the Golconda Saloon. It occurred to him that he should get up, that he had a man to kill. The gunman was mystified as to why his muscles refused to respond to his mind's demand. He should close his eyes. He could feel a fleck of sawdust in one. A thing like that can spoil a man's aim. Drat it, John would be mad as a scalded weasel, for he'd set store by Chinee and this hombre had up and killed him. It was Jacob's final thought.

Dancer sheathed his sidearm as the fast gun from Texas breathed his last.

"That's the price of glory, bad man."

As the smoke cleared, a timid cheer started among the sparse group of witnesses in the saloon, growing in volume and enthusiasm as it became apparent to all that the occupation of Raindance by armed force was at an end. Mulroney slapped the bar in boisterous relief.

"Drinks are on the house!"

Dancer was on his knees, cradling Macklin's head in his lap. He pressed his neckerchief against the right side of the rancher's skull where the Tarantula's bullet had plowed a deep bloody furrow. He had bled like a hog stuck for butchering, but no serious damage had been done, save a colossal headache. Macklin was struggling and fussing to get up.

"Just lay there a minute, partner. Let's have the saw-bones take a look at that hardrock skull of yours."

"I'm all right, let me up. Is it over?"

"This part of it, I reckon. You hollering when you did and the lead you threw at that hombre on the stairs saved my bacon. Thanks."

The doctor, who had been working on the Indian, walked over then. He was a youngish man of indistinguishable age and unremarkable features, haggard beyond his years, but with a gentleness about him and the twinkle of good humor in his pale eyes. His clothes were fashionable, but rumpled, and he wore a stovepipe hat. His sleeves were rolled up and his slender but sinuous forearms were caked with blood. He spoke with the clipped cadence of a New Englander. He waggled a bony thumb over his shoulder at the wounded Apache lying across the room.

"That one will live perhaps, but I wager he'll tweet like a bird the rest of his days. Shot away his sociability." The doctor chuckled. "No helping the other two, of course. Now, let's have a look at that head, Macklin."

Dancer relinquished the care of his wounded friend to the doctor and stepped quickly to the bar. He paused briefly to watch four men struggling out the door with Chinee's bulky and cumbersome carcass, then called out to Mulroney.

"Yes, sir. Anything *you* wish is on the house . . . tonight or any night. I never seen the like of what you done, Mr.?"

"Dancer."

The bartender looked taken aback at the familiar ring of the name.

"Sure, sure. You're the man they had on trial here in the saloon. Gonna hang for killin' Macklin. Well, I'm sure enough glad that's all square now, Mr. Dancer. What'll it be? Whiskey? Or we have some fine brandy in the back . . . I—"

"Later," Dancer said, interrupting, "where's Blaine?"

"Oh m'lord!" Mulroney gasped, his face paling. "In all the excitement the poor man slipped my mind."

The bartender hastily peeled off his apron and rushed around the end of the bar.

"This way, Mr. Dancer . . . I'm afraid of what we'll find. We heard such hideous cries."

Dancer was confused. As he followed the scurrying bartender to the stairs he asked, "What do you mean?"

"The Blackthorns had him tortured. No one knows why," Mulroney replied over his shoulder.

The big Irishman took three steps at a time, Dancer on his heels, gun drawn. They burst through the door to the gambler's quarters.

Dancer veered to avoid a collision when Mulroney stopped dead in his tracks just inside the door. A gasp of horror and revulsion escaped the barkeep's throat as he wheeled and fled the room. Once free of the threshold he fell to his knees, retching convulsively.

Jack fought down the bile rising in his own throat as he surveyed the gruesome scene before him. The floors and walls were splattered with gore, giving the place the appearance and stench of a slaughterhouse. The hunter of men had encountered his share of atrocities in his travels across an oftentimes savage frontier, so he knew the nature of the agonies that had been inflicted upon the suffering wretch bound to the chair in front of him.

"Blaine?"

The bloodied creature jerkily raised a head marred beyond recognition and attempted to focus on the strange voice before him.

"M–my . . . gold. S–save . . . my . . . gold."

"Blaine. Listen to me. Linda Macklin. Where is Linda?"

"Linda. She . . . she loved the . . . the flowers."

"Where is she? Where have Worthy and Stone Wolf taken her?"

"Help me."

"Not until you tell me where Linda is being held. Tell me where she is, Blaine, then I'll help you."

Slowly, methodically, Dancer prompted the pain–crazed gambler into revealing the location of the hideaway. Then he rose to leave.

"Wait! Don't go. Blackthorns after my gold. Kill . . . them for me. Don't let them have my gold. Buried . . . on the Macklin ranch. Kill them. My gold. Mine."

"Stolen gold, Blaine, bought with blood. Your gold has likely cost you your life."

Dancer dug a knife from the pocket of his denims, folded out the blade and cut the bonds that held Blaine to the chair. Blaine teetered, then fell to the floor, moaning.

"Please, kill me. Can't . . . stand any more . . . I beg you. Kill me."

Dancer looked at the pitiful remnant of the man at his feet. He glanced around the room, his eyes halting on a small glistening object atop the bureau. He stepped to pick up Blaine's sleeve pistol, checked the load, then bent to place the gun in the quivering palm of the former marauder. He placed Blaine's bloody fingers around the small weapon, one in the trigger guard, and walked from the room.

As Dancer descended the stairway to the saloon below, a shot rang out behind him. His pace faltered a moment, then, without turning, he continued down the steps.

Macklin was sitting in a chair, grumbling as the doctor stood over him to put the finishing touches to a bandage that swathed his head. The rancher flinched, emitting an oath as the medical man pulled the last knot tight.

"How you feeling, Rad?" asked Dancer as he approached.

Macklin nodded and pulled away from the hovering ministrations of the doctor. "Blaine. Did you find him?" he asked. "What was that shot?"

"If you're feeling up to it, let's go get Linda."

The site for the kidnappers' hideout had been craftily chosen. The cabin was set back into a deep cleft in the mountainside, making it virtually inaccessible from three sides. The area in front was cleared of trees and brush for a good two hundred yards, eliminating cover for any attacker, exposing any aggressor to fire. The walls of the rustic structure were fashioned of heavy logs; the door and the shutter on the lone window were of heavy planking—too formidable for any bullet to penetrate. Both shutter and door were slotted in the shape of a cross, enabling a defender inside the cabin to cover the entire clearing from a single firing position.

Dancer and Macklin crouched near the edge of the forest, carefully regarding the enemy camp, studying the setting in search of a strategic approach.

"This could be a real chore, Rad. Whoever put that layout together wasn't long on socializing. A gnat would be hard pressed to sneak in there without being shot full of holes."

Jack pointed toward the corral fifty yards upslope of the shack.

"Just two horses. The appaloosa is missing. Means Worthy must be in there alone with Linda."

Macklin's jaw tightened and his eyes narrowed as he wiped a sleeve across his mouth. His face turned crimson.

"How we going to get in there, Jack? We've got to get my little girl out of there . . . now."

He started to rise.

Dancer clapped a strong hand sternly on the rancher's shoulder, scolding him with his eyes.

"Don't get rattled, partner. Linda has been captive for days. Whatever was to happen to her has happened already. If we go off half-cocked now, we'll only get her killed.

"I know it's ripping at your innards not to charge in there, believe me. It galls me for her to be in there too. But we must do this right the first time. We aren't apt to get another chance."

Macklin slumped back to squat on his heels, rubbing a callused palm across his face.

"Sorry, son. You're right, of course. You make the call. Just tell me what to do."

Blowing into cupped hands to warm them, Dancer resumed his watchful posture, scrutinizing the clearing, the cabin, the surrounding terrain—groping through his instincts, experiences and fund of knowledge for a feasible method with which to breach the defenses of the outlaw stronghold.

The mountain morning was clear and crisp, and a ground fog hung hip-high across the empty expanse between their position and their target. A lazy tendril of smoke raised from the stone chimney of the cabin.

It occurred to the woodswise hunter of men that he might make his way on his belly under cover of the thinning fog. But once at the cabin, how would he gain entrance or force Worthy into the open? No, it was too chancy. Suddenly his eyes brightened and he slapped Macklin on the arm.

"Here's how we work it, amigo.

"I'm going to circle around to get up on that slope behind the house. I can throw a rope around a tree and let myself down onto the roof. Then I'll stuff a blanket in the chimney to plug it. There is enough of a fire going in there it should smoke up the place good and proper. That ought to bring Worthy outside to investigate.

"You position yourself right here and stay under cover. Once Worthy is outside, *cut him down!* Take your time, make sure he's well clear of the door before you shoot so he won't dart back inside. And Rad, make your first shot count. We don't want to crawl in any holes after a wounded lobo."

"There's a steep pitch to that roof, Jack, and those shingles are covered with moss. It'll be slicker than spit on a doorknob up there. What if you slip and fall, making a racket? Worthy would know something's up for sure then. He might even kill her."

"Anything we do will have some risk involved, my friend. I'll go slow and easy, being careful not to slip. Besides, I don't reckon he would dare to harm Linda while under siege. He'd have to figure her to be a bargaining chip for him . . . a way out.

"But if you don't want to do it this way, come up with a better plan. I'm sure enough open to suggestions."

"I don't have an alternative. I'm just plumb scared out of my skull for Linda."

"Yep, so am I. But I've got to think that our chances of success are better now than later. No telling when Stone Wolf will show back up here. If we wait until he returns, I don't know how we would get her away from the two of them, unharmed. I say we go for it."

Macklin nodded, extending his right hand. Dancer took it, held it firmly a moment then melted away into the trees.

The rancher sat for what seemed to him an agonizingly lengthy period of time, alternately straining his eyes against the spot on the sheer slope above the cabin where Jack Dancer must appear and watching the hateful door which separated him from his daughter. Then he spotted the man in black, looking smaller in the distance than he had expected. He watched with bated breath as Dancer circled the sturdy girth of a towering fir with his lasso, then affixed the other end around his waist.

Dancer started down, hand over hand, moccasined feet pushing alternately against the steep, craggy face of the mountain. A shower of pebbles dislodged by the pressure of a foot fell cascading onto the roof below. He halted, poised in midair, holding his breath. When no reaction was forth-coming from the occupants of the cabin, he continued his cautious descent.

As Jack reached the rooftop he paused, crouching, untied the rope from around his waist, then slowly stood erect, test-ing the surface beneath his feet. Painstakingly and noise-lessly, he made his way up the aging, moss-shagged, shin-gled slope to the ridge of the roof, then scampered like a squirrel along the ridge to the chimney. He loosed the blan-ket held around his neck with a rawhide piggin string and stuffed it into the flue of the smoking chimney. He waited a sufficient time to be certain the escape of smoke from the fireplace below was effectively stilled, then backed down further onto the slope of the roof, away from the cabin door and out of sight.

The minutes passed slowly. Across the clearing, Macklin hunkered down behind a lichen-encrusted boulder, Winchester trained on the plank door, his brow beaded with perspiration despite the coolness of the morning air. Dancer crouched on the roof like a coiled spring, .44 in his hand.

A crack appeared at the door. Smoke rushed eagerly from the black slit, hell bent for the reaches of the trees on the mountain slope above. The door swung wide and a murky form materialized from the smoky interior.

Manfred Worthy warily descended the pair of steps to the ground, holding his blanket-draped captive with one hairy forearm across her neck. He stood with his back to the cabin using the girl in his grasp to shield him against possible dan-ger while he searched the clearing with weeping eyes for any sign of intrusion. Apparently satisfied, but still clutching Linda Macklin before him, the outlaw backed away from the front wall of the house to gain a view of the offending chimney.

Macklin had his rifle trained on a spot midway between

the shoulders of the kidnapper's broad back. His finger took up slack on the trigger. He took a deep breath and held it.

He could not shoot! He was afraid the bullet might pass through the man's body and strike his daughter.

Rad Macklin stepped from concealment into the clearing, walking with grim determination toward Worthy and Linda, rifle at the ready. Sensing the presence at his back, Worthy turned, dragging his human shield before him.

"Worthy, curse your mangy hide, I have come for my daughter. Let her go!"

"You come for a bullet, old man."

The renegade raised his pistol, holding Linda tightly in front of him. Dancer dropped like a whisper from the eave of the roof to the ground between Worthy and the cabin.

"Drop it, coyote. You're covered."

A look of panic darkened Worthy's swarthy features like clouds moving across the moon. He whipped sideways between his two enemies, placing the muzzle of his sixgun against the temple of his captive. Linda displayed no fear, no emotion, seemingly calm in the crisis.

"This need not come to killing, Worthy," Dancer told him. "Let the girl go. I'll give you an hour start before I come after you."

"Hah. Not likely. I ain't buyin'. Now both of you, drop your weapons or I'll blow the little lady's head off. Now!"

Macklin hastily shed his rifle. As he did, Linda let her body go limp, a dead weight in the outlaw's grasp. Worthy faltered. The barrel of his gun strayed for but a fraction of a second. It was long enough.

The crashing report of Dancer's .44 leapt across the clearing, resounding in the trees. The bullet entered directly between Manfred Worthy's eyes and sent his wire-rimmed spectacles spinning into the air.

The echo of gunfire faded.

A solitary crystal tear made its way hesitantly down Linda's cheek as Rad Macklin swept his daughter into his arms. They stood, unmoving, unspeaking, holding each other.

After a time, Dancer approached them leading three horses. He cleared his throat to keep his voice from cracking.

"Let's go home."

Chapter Sixteen

They made their way down the heavily wooded slope, three survivors of a taut encounter of guile, grit and gunsmoke on the mountain.

Sitting the blood bay, Dancer fronted the small and silent column, picking a path toward town. The sagging, forlorn form of Linda Macklin followed, draped in Jack's outsized mackinaw. And as close behind her as he could crowd without sharing her saddle rode a relieved but deeply concerned father.

Nor was their retreat unobserved, for as the forest swallowed them, the appaloosa stepped from cover across the clearing, a stoic Stone Wolf astride its back watching the trio head away. The Indian had returned from town in time to see the firefight in front of the cabin. Disinclined to join the fray, he had watched from the shielding foliage as Worthy fell victim to the relentless gun of Jack Dancer. Now he reined the horse to a halt above the body of his hapless saddlemate and companion in crime. Manfred Worthy lay covered by the blanket discarded by the rescued captive. There was no glint of empathy or pity or sense of loss in the half-breed's eyes—only scornful disgust at the dead man's ineptitude.

Stone Wolf dismissed the corpse and stepped into the smoky interior of the cabin. A quick glimpse with hawk-keen eyes netted nothing he cared to carry away, so he snatched up the near-empty bottle of sour mash from the table, then deposited himself on the stoop to consider his next action.

Moving like a shadow, Stone Wolf had been an inconspicuous witness to the dramatic events of the last two days in Raindance. He had heard the Apache, Tarantula, disclose the location of a fortune in gold to Peaceable John Blackthorn. He had seen two of the Blackthorns, accompanied by that horribly disfigured and disheveled little man, leave town in empty wagons, ostensibly to retrieve the gold. And, peering over the curved tops of the batwing doors of the Golconda, he had watched with grudging admiration as the man called Dancer effectively and efficiently eliminated in turn the Oriental, the Apache and the gunman, Jacob Blackthorn, with workmanlike precision. He heard the shot that the tortured gambler, Blaine, dispatched into his own brain—and he saw the sheet-draped body of his former employer carried from the saloon. All these things Stone Wolf had seen and heard, and they all were of interest to him to the degree that they applied to his own personal well-being and fortunes.

After draining the bottle of whiskey, the half-breed tossed it aside, watching it roll to a halt against the blanket shroud of Manfred Worthy. He rubbed a fringed buckskin sleeve across his lips and began to rise, knowing now what he must do.

Stone Wolf decided to travel immediately to the Flying M ranch. The Blackthorns were interlopers, latecomers to the situation. Only he, Stone Wolf, deserved to fall heir to Court Blaine's golden treasure. He must contrive to join these Blackthorns, ingratiate himself with them, then somehow secure the spoils for himself.

Of course, the old man, Macklin, and the girl must be eliminated. If left alive, they would stir up the whole of Colorado against him for his part in the abduction and outrageous assaults upon Linda Macklin, leaving him little freedom to spend his spoils. They must die.

And most importantly, Stone Wolf must kill the man, Dancer. The hunter of men would mount a tenacious pursuit for his capture, of course. But fear of capture was not the motivation for the half-breed's brooding and murderous intent. This had become a matter of personal honor and pride. Stone Wolf must face Dancer in combat and emerge the victor, the greatest warrior. He had known it must be so since he first had seen the man in black aboard the magnificent appaloosa stallion that day in the ranchyard of the Flying M. He knew it when the man reemerged, still alive after the ambush at the ranch. He knew it when he saw the violent showdown in the Golconda Saloon. And he knew it again this day as he watched Dancer outwit and outduel Manfred Worthy to rescue the woman. It was a thing destined to be, this battle of warriors, and Stone Wolf awaited the confrontation with relish.

The Indian stayed to the backtrails of the high country, pushing the spotted-rump steed in a circuitous route toward the Flying M ranch, avoiding the pockets of population around the valley community of Raindance.

From the same high bluff where he had fired his bullet into the broad back of Jack Dancer, Stone Wolf observed the treasure seekers at work in the ranchyard below. He smiled inwardly as he picked his way down the slope to join them.

Working knee deep in the ooze of mud and ashes where once stood the Macklin home, the fortune hunters looked like animated clay sculptures, coated with the residue of their labors. They sloshed about extricating slime, rocks and nuggets by the bucketsful, so intent upon their task and so consumed by the fever of riches that they failed to notice the bronzed rider watching them from a few feet away. Stone Wolf considered killing them where they stood, but the thought of the physical task of salvaging the gold himself kept his finger from the trigger of the rifle resting in the crook of his sinewy arm. "Hao," he said.

The slime-slicked men scrambled for their guns, slipping and falling in the muddy morass. The Indian spread his arms palms up, a gesture of peaceful intent.

"I come as a friend to offer you the power of my gun. You will have need of me before the sun goes behind the mountain."

"I don't know who you be, breed," Peaceable John replied while covering the intruder with the long barrel of his Colt, "but we don't need no more firepower, and we don't need no friend the likes of you."

"I could have killed you as you wallowed in the mud like a pig," Stone Wolf said. "You let gold cloud your mind. Go back to your digging. I will watch for you."

"Gold? How'd you . . . what gold you talkin' about? There ain't no gold here," said Caleb Free.

Stone Wolf just smiled.

"You planting corn, then? I will watch for you."

"We need anybody to stand guard, we got more and better folks in town," John Blackthorn said.

"You have no one. Dead men have no eyes to see."

"Wh . . . what? What are you talkin' about, you red heathen?"

"Your brother and the big, ugly one are dead. The Apache lies dying."

"He's lyin', John," Jedidiah cried.

"How'd they get dead?" Peaceable John asked, not believing, but suddenly afraid.

So Stone Wolf told them of the saloon battle and of Dancer's clean harvest of their brother and their hired killers. Peaceable John Blackthorn slumped to the ground, visibly shaken.

"Let's go see for ourselves, John," his brother urged with a whine. "I ain't ready to take this ragtail breed's word for nothin'. He's tryin' to fool us away from here. There ain't a man alive could of faced Jacob with a gun and come away upright, let alone them other two to boot. He is lying, I tell you. Let's kill him and go back to town."

"Who killed them?" John asked.

"A man called Dancer."

"Jack Dancer?" John said, startled.

Stone Wolf shrugged, not knowing the manhunter's given name.

"You know him, John?" Jedidiah asked, not liking the stricken look on his brother's face.

"I know of him."

"Could I speak to you alone, Mr. Macklin?"

The doctor's face was a study in solemnity as he closed the door of the examining room behind him. Macklin reached across Dancer's broad chest, stopping him as he turned to leave.

"Mr. Dancer is a good friend, Doc. He's the one got my daughter back. Whatever you've got to say concerns us both."

"Very well," the doctor replied uncomfortably. "Linda has been badly used, as you've seen for yourselves. She is bruised head to toe. Beaten. Manhandled."

The physician looked away, shying from the agony in the rancher's eyes. Finally he continued.

"Physically . . . she will recover, rapidly I would suppose. She is young. She's healthy.

"But gentlemen, do you have any concept of the devastating impact a thing like this has on a woman? Linda has been forced through an emotional meat grinder. She will require all your tenderness, all your understanding. Most of all, you must be patient.

"She will likely have periods of melancholy, fits of anger over meaningless trifles, horrible nightmares.

"I cannot say when Linda may be herself again. With tender care, and in time . . ."

Macklin grabbed him by the lapels. "But she will be all right, won't she Doc?"

"That's up to her, Rad. Only her. I've known the hardiest of women, pioneer stock, even *fallen women* that have been decimated by an experience like this. You can imagine how much more difficult it will be for a decent young woman of breeding, like Linda, to endure such a burden."

Dancer and Macklin looked at one another, each sharing the same deep concern.

"It would help to leave here," the doctor suggested. "Get her as far from this country as you can, as fast as you can. There is nothing here for Linda but bad memories.

"People will talk, too, I am afraid. A thing like this invites sordid speculation. Unfair as it certainly is, people will talk. Many will be understanding, but will say wrong things despite their good intentions. Others may be outright cruel and thoughtless. There will be knowing glances. Whispered asides. Gutter humor. Crude remarks.

"I tell you these things not to alarm you, frighten you or hurt you, Rad. You know that. I tell you because I have seen it all before in a dozen other towns like Raindance.

"There's one more thing," the doctor said, frowning. "I would advise you to watch your daughter very closely. Someone should be near her at all times, night and day."

"I don't understand, Doc. Why?"

"She may very well try to take her own life."

Jack and Rad escorted Linda to the hotel for a hot bath and to allow her access to her wardrobe. She seemed subdued, but otherwise normal. She had shed no tears since they had brought her down from the mountain.

They waited for her in Rad Macklin's room, talking and sharing a pot of coffee.

"Rad, partner, after I've talked to Linda I'll be riding out to the ranch. Quint will want to know she's safe and we need to know what, if anything, has been going on out there. You stay and keep an eye on your daughter. She needs you now. Quint and I can handle any trouble."

"Jack, what about the rest of that Blackthorn outfit? They will be after your hide with a vengeance when they learn what happened in the saloon last night. They are bound to come shooting."

"I've found that the quickest way out of trouble is to face it. Don't you worry about me. You look to Linda.

"Stay off the street if you can, and go armed. The Blackthorns will know that you were in on that ruckus with me. They could come for you, too, if they get by me."

Both men's heads jerked around at a gentle rap at the door. Linda stepped meekly into the room, looking as beautiful as Dancer had ever seen her. He stepped forward to greet her, gently placing his hands on her upper arms. She recoiled, jumped back and dropped her gaze to the floor. She rubbed her arms to rid herself of his touch. Dancer retreated from her, stuffing the offending hands into the back pockets of his denims.

"My, don't you look pretty," Macklin said brightly. "Did you enjoy your bath, honey?"

Linda looked up at her father as her eyes filled with tears.

"Daddy, I . . . I couldn't get clean."

Chapter Seventeen

Dawn was just a promise when Dancer mounted the bay and headed out of town. A venomous black rage was building inside the man—a festering anger toward that entire breed of men who choose to run roughshod through life, inflicting their wills upon others by brute force to satisfy their grasping greeds and animal lusts.

Linda's reaction to his touch had struck Jack like a mortar shell to the heart. She had recoiled in fear and revulsion as he reached out offering love and tender support.

All the while during the bloody events leading up to the moment of her rescue on the mountain, Jack's mind had been weaving an idyllic fantasy of a life with Linda as his wife. A life of serenity and joy and home on his ranch on the Gunnison, with a howling pack of little Dancers running through green meadows where ponies frolicked. Now that dream had been shattered, a victim of the bestial violations perpetrated upon an innocent girl by gold-crazed, evil men. Ruined lives!

As he rode, Dancer struggled to rein his fury. Gunplay loomed imminent and he, more than most men, was aware of the need for a cool head and a clear mind in such instances. Anger and anxiety have no place on the field of battle. Those he knew who had carried such emotions into combat were mostly dead. By the time he reached the vicinity of the ranch, he was once again the calm, controlled hunter of men.

Quint Hawkes knelt in heavy cover, peering at the activity on the floor of the valley beneath his vista. He turned to reach for his saddlebags and found his nose at Jack's knee.

"Whoa! . . . Dancer, you scared me plumb into next year. Don't never sneak up on a man thataway. How'd you find me, anyhow?"

Dancer shook his head and chuckled.

"I've followed herds of longhorn cattle that didn't leave the trail you did, Quint."

"Well, I never laid claim to being Kit Carson. Never mind that," he said with a strange light in his eyes, "come see what that bunch down there has hauled out of a hole in the ground. More gold than a man could spend in a dozen lifetimes, Dancer. It was buried right under the ranchhouse all this time. Can you believe it? We were sitting on a king's fortune. They got both wagons full and it looks like they've only just got started."

Jack looked at him queerly.

"Aren't you curious about Linda, Quint? Aren't you wondering what happened?"

"Huh? Oh . . . sure. Is Linda all right? Did you find her?"

"We found her. She's alive, but she has been through a terrible ordeal."

Jack knelt down and began to pull together the makings of a fire to brew coffee. Quint Hawkes stepped across to glance down again at the Blackthorn work party.

"I'll keep an eye on these hombres while you tell me all about it. Is Rad in one piece? What happened?"

So Dancer relived the saga of the search for Linda Macklin,

from the time he had last seen the lanky foreman of the Flying M. In the telling he felt again the surge of emotions, the pain and fear and glory. His voice cracked as he related the treatment Linda had been forced to endure at the hands of her captors. He gritted his teeth as he recalled the killings.

At some point during Jack's recounting of events, Hawkes had surrendered his watchpost and sat cross-legged facing the man in black, rapt with attention.

"When this is through," Dancer said, indicating the gold scavengers in the valley with a sweep of his finger, "I'll be going after Stone Wolf. He is the last of them, and the worst."

"You may not have to go far, partner. He was down there yesterday, with them others."

Dancer poured their tin cups full of coffee, then drenched the hand-sized fire with the rest of the pot, sending up a sizzling cloud of steam.

"We'd best be moving then. If that Indian's about, he'll spot us here, if he hasn't already, and I'd just as leave than see him first."

They packed up and moved swiftly into the deeper sanctuary of the forest to plan their attack.

Dancer crouched in the depression of an old creek bed muddy from recent rains, at the foot of a steep bluff overlooking the ranchyard. Suddenly he realized that he was hidden in the same dry watercourse where he had landed after being shot from ambush by the half-breed, Stone Wolf. He smiled to himself. Old habits are hard to break.

The Blackthorn brothers, Peaceable John and Jedidiah, Caleb Free and their new cohort, Stone Wolf, lay in their bedrolls near the diggings. Dancer had watched as the men grudgingly quit the gold salvage to eat a light supper and turn in, anxious for the dawn, so to begin again. Stone Wolf had appeared from somewhere up the valley as they sat around the cookfire and he joined them for beans and coffee. But when the others rolled into their blankets, the half-breed withdrew into the darkness, preferring a solitary bed away from the camp and the light of the fire. Dancer appreciated this show of caution and logic. He knew that the Indian remained at hand, however, because he could make out the faint form of the appaloosa tethered in the darkness on the other side of the camp.

Jack leaned back, relaxing as best he could in the muddy draw, pulling his hat down to his nose. He yawned and closed his eyes, determined to take advantage of this period of waiting to get a little rest, for all hell would break loose in the morning.

Dancer was a man who had never become inured to killing another man. He had never become jaded to the experience of looking upon the dead. Each time he slipped his gun back into its sheath, he prayed it would remain there. Without exception, he was gripped by nausea and regret at the taking of a human life, no matter how necessary the action or how vile that life had become. He considered it his curse that he had been thrust into the role of a slayer of men by possessing the talents of grit, guile and gunspeed. Yet, when called upon to right a brutal wrong or to protect an innocent victim, he found himself unable to lay aside his guns. Jack Dancer was a reluctant but vital instrument of an untamed era in the West.

He had sent Hawkes around to the other side of the valley with instructions to close in on the outlaw camp just before first light. They would approach the target from two directions, hopefully to surprise the enemy at their breakfast chores. They planned to take them alive, if the renegades would allow it.

A whicker from one of the horses brought Dancer alert. He heard the camp begin to stir. The false dawn was starless and he could scarcely make out the forms of the men as, one by one, they climbed from their night beds. One man disappeared in the gloom to Jack's right. He could hear the rattle of dry brush as the man sought a moment of privacy. As he heard the man returning, Dancer crept forward, out of the creek bed onto the flat.

Dancer knew that his black clothing and sun-darkened complexion would render him practically invisible in the faint predawn light. He advanced in a low crouch, rifle poised and cocked, one .44 in its holster, the other in his belt. He said a little prayer to the gods that Hawkes was advancing simultaneously.

"Hold fast," Dancer called out, standing to cover the camp, "and keep your hands clear of your weapons! We've got you boxed!"

The four men froze, complete surprise common on their faces in the faint, flickering reflections of the newly ignited cookfire. The campsite brightened as the wood of the fire caught, blazing higher.

"Who in blazes? What do you want here, mister? We're just down-at-the-heels cowherders, mindin' our own business," Peaceable John said, lying as smoothly as he could manage on such short notice. "We got nothin' of value, but you're welcome to some breakfast beans if you're hungry."

"I'm taking you in, Blackthorn. All of you."

Stone Wolf stepped closer to the fire. The flames cast glistening shards of light across the rugged, muscular topography of his bare chest.

"This is the man Dancer," the half-breed announced, "the great killer."

"Dancer?" Jedidiah screamed. "You kilt my brother, you highbindin', murderin' . . ." He went for his gun.

Jedidiah Blackthorn's finger jerked the trigger of the big Colt as the two .44 slugs from Dancer's rifle tore through his chest. The outlaw's gun did not clear the holster, but sent a bullet plowing into his own leg.

Dancer leapt to the side before the dead renegade hit the ground, a shot from the smoking muzzle of Caleb Free's sidearm whistling past his ear as he fell and rolled. He dropped the rifle and the .44 Colt was bucking in his hand. A strange, strained cry escaped the puckered aperture that served as Free's mouth as he fell into the fire, gutshot.

Dancer scurried backward out of the firelight, searching the shadows for the other two gunmen. Where was Hawkes? Why wasn't he joining the fray?

Jack dropped behind a charred beam in the burned-out rubble near the excavation. He peered over the top.

A cloud of black charcoal exploded in Dancer's face, filling his eyes with soot as the shot from John Blackthorn's gun plowed a deep groove across the top of the sheltering timber. Jack rolled onto his back, swiping at his eyes with the back of his hand.

Dancer felt the rapid pounding of approaching booted feet vibrate the ground beneath his back. He flipped over and groped for his pistol. Through blurred vision he saw the form of a man poised above him. Peaceable John spoke in a thundering voice choked with rage.

"You've kilt my family, gunfighter, but the Blackthorn name will outlive yourn!"

The hovering outlaw loosed a shot as Dancer drew the gun from his belt, firing blindly. A searing pain tore through the prone manhunter's shoulder. Darkness fell across his face, followed by a crushing impact. His head reeled. He could not breathe. He fought the smothering weight, struggling to crawl free.

The muffled sounds of faraway gunfire filtered through the forest to reach the ears of Many Ponies. He held up a hand, halting the five Ute braves that followed in single file. It had been a good hunt and the pack ponies labored under heavy loads of elk and bear meat on their backs.

Many Ponies twisted around on his paint horse to summon the young man at the end of the column, who rode quickly forward.

"The sounds of angry guns come from the east. I will take Walking Bear and Gray Cloud with me to see the trouble. You will lead the others to the village with the kill from the hunt."

"That way lies the white man's land. It is white man's trouble, none of ours."

"This land, all this land, is my home. We will go to see."

Dancer leaned on one elbow, panting and sickened, having escaped from beneath the lifeless body of John Blackthorn. His vision cleared, but the searing pain in his left shoulder hurt like thunder. He retched, spewing the bitter contents of his stomach across the uncaring cadaver lying at his side.

"Dancer. Dancer."

Quint Hawkes came rushing up.

"You all right, partner?"

"No, I'm not all right. I'm shot. Where the dickens you been, Hawkes?"

"Things happened so fast I couldn't get off a clear shot. I was scared I might hit you."

"Never mind, stay alert. Stone Wolf is still out there."

"No he ain't. He took off on that spotted horse of yours as soon as the shootin' started. I flung a couple of shots at him, but he got clean away, I reckon.

"Let me have a look at that shoulder."

Hawkes took the pistol from Dancer's hand and stuck it in his own belt. He bent over the wounded manhunter, tearing the shirt away from the wound.

"Ooowee, that looks nasty, old pard."

Quint dabbed at the wound with a scrap of cloth he had torn from the tail of Jack's blood-soaked shirt.

"Looks as if she went on through. Missed the bone, but it's tore up in there.

"You want me to ride for the doc, or do you want to try to sit a horse?"

The cowboy took the bandanna from around his neck and pressed it firmly into the wound, stemming the flow of blood.

"I'll make it," Dancer replied, sitting up and wincing at the pain. "Find my other guns for me, will you? I think I'd best sit right here for a spell."

"Dancer . . ."

Hawkes hesitated, a grin starting at the corners of his mouth.

"What?"

"You seen the gold, didn't you?"

"So?"

"So we're rich, man. We don't have to hit it another lick the rest of our lives, either of us."

Hawkes was laughing and cavorting, clapping his hands.

"What's got into you, Quint? Calm down, now. That's not our gold, not a nugget of it. It belongs to those miners in Climax, the ones Jubal Blackthorn took it from.

"There may be a reward of some sort coming for the recovery of the shipment, but that ought to go to Rad Macklin. He'll need it to start over."

"You crazy, Jack? Those miners gave that gold up for lost long ago. It's ours by rights for finding it. We're rich, partner . . . filthy rich!"

Astounded, Dancer looked at his friend. The light of greed burned brightly in the man's eyes, a look of obsession twisted his features.

"Bring me my horse, Quint. We aren't keeping that gold."

Hawkes drew the manhunter's pistol from his belt and

pulled back the hammer. He pointed the barrel at a spot between the wounded man's eyes.

"You going to kill me, Quint?" Dancer asked calmly.

"I got no choice, partner. Seems you just won't have it any other way. 'Course I'll tell folks one of these hombres done it.

"Sorry, friend. It goes against my grain to do this. But Dancer, I been dirt poor all my born days. Shucks, man, I never even owned a horse of my own. Ever' broomtail I ever forked was wearing the brand of the outfit I worked for.

"I'll give you a decent burial, Dancer, after I move the gold. No hard feelin's."

The cowhand's finger tightened on the trigger. Dancer sat helpless, staring into the dark bore of a gun barrel that looked as big as a tin plate.

A whirring sound sliced into the morning calm, followed by a solid thump. Hawkes lowered the barrel of the pistol and bent down his chin to watch the dark, spreading stain on the front of his shirt. He looked questioningly at Dancer, then his eyes clouded and he pitched forward onto the ground, a Ute hunting arrow protruding from between his shoulder blades.

The Indians advanced their ponies at a walk. One lean, lithe brave, the leader of the group, stretched an open palm toward the sky.

"Dancer . . . you have been busy this day, my brother."

Jack recognized the young warrior—Many Ponies, a war chief of the Uncompahgre Ute and cousin to Fire Cloud, the Indian boy whom Dancer had nursed in the wilderness and returned to his people.

Many Ponies had been sitting next to Jack the night that he had been adopted into the tribe. Following the feast celebrating Fire Cloud's return, the two men had visited well into the night and had become fast friends.

"Many Ponies, your coming is most welcome, my brother, and most timely. I am in your debt."

"It is a small thing."

Dancer struggled to his feet. Shaking his head, he bent to pluck his Colt from the limp fingers of Quint Hawkes.

"So long . . . partner."

Chapter Eighteen

Using the strong and supple branches of aspen from the adjoining forest, the Utes fashioned a travois upon which to transport their blood brother to the white medicine man in Raindance.

Many Ponies assured Dancer that, while his battle wound healed, no man would trespass upon the valley. The heavy rocks that sparkle in the sun would be as he left them. The Ute would guard the gold for their friend and brother.

Dancer told the Utes to take the teams and saddle horses that the slain outlaws had left behind for themselves. Many Ponies was pleased. His tribal status would be greatly elevated to bring home such a prize.

The bodies of the Blackthorn brothers and Caleb Free were dumped unceremoniously into an unmarked common grave, but Dancer said words over the singular grave of Quint Hawkes. Quint had not been a bad man, just a vulnerable one. The cowboy had fallen victim to the seduction of unearned and sudden riches. Dancer had seen more than one good man felled by gold fever. He would tell it so that Hawkes had been killed by the Blackthorns, fighting for the Flying M. The Macklins should not suffer the added grief of

172

a friend gone bad. Nor did Jack want to involve the Utes. A great many people in Colorado, for whom old wounds still festered, would not accept the killing of a white man by an Indian, no matter how just the cause. It was better this way.

The burying done, Many Ponies strapped Jack to the travois behind the blood bay for the trip over the rutted road to Raindance.

The combined effects of a stiff dose of laudanum and the trauma resulting from his shoulder wound caused Jack Dancer to sleep the clock twice around. When he awoke, she was sitting at his bedside.

"Linda."

"Hello, Jack. How do you feel?"

"Too lightheaded to know just yet, thanks. I'll be all right . . . I've proven to be a quick healer."

"You've done so much for us, Dad and me, and it has cost you so dearly. We shall never be able to repay you."

"That's mighty close to an insult, young lady. There is nothing to repay. I only did what one friend does for another."

"Still, we are grateful. I am grateful."

"That I accept," he said, smiling. Then he sobered. "How are *you* doing, Linda?"

She looked down at her hands in her lap, nervously twisting a hanky.

"I'm feeling well, I suppose."

"Good! Because I want you to shake out one of those pretty little dresses you wear and have it ready to hand. When I climb up out of this featherbed, I'm going to come calling."

Linda looked up in alarm.

"Oh, no, Jack . . . I—"

"I love you. I want you to be my wife."

Linda Macklin's eyes welled with tears.

"You can't, Jack, don't you realize that? My name is forever soiled. No matter what really did or did not happen when those horrible men took me, people will think and say the worst."

Dancer's face darkened and he sat up in bed, screwing his face into a mask of pain. He steadied himself and spoke through gritted teeth.

"I'd horsewhip the man who would speak against you.

"Sure, you've been hurt. Victimized. No one can deny it. I deplore what happened to you because it has caused you pain. But Linda, honey, what you've been through does not lessen you in my eyes, nor does it diminish the depth of my love for you. You are the same wonderful woman you were before. You are the victim of a vicious crime, the same as your daddy was a victim when Patch shot him. Don't you see that?"

"Yes, I know you're right, Jack.

"I know it, but I can't feel it, not yet. Someday, maybe. If I could marry anyone, be with anyone, I would want it to be you, my sweet. I loved you before those men took me . . . and I suppose I love you still. But all my tender feelings have been buried. I can't reach them.

"The thought of *any* man touching me . . . I just cannot."

"I would never force matters. I can give you time, Linda . . . all the time you need."

She shook her head vehemently, then straightened, assuming a formal air.

"Daddy and I are leaving . . . to travel in the East for a time. St. Louis, Chicago, Washington City."

Linda rose, reached to squeeze Jack's hand, then turned to leave.

"Linda."

She paused with her hand on the doorknob, turning tear-filled eyes to gaze back at him.

"When you are ready," Dancer said, "you know how to get in touch."

He blew a kiss off the flat of his palm as she drew the door closed behind her.

The owners of the Climax mines traveled en masse to Raindance to express their appreciation, baffled but ecstatic at the unexpected and intact return of the stolen shipment of high-grade ore. They were in extremely generous and phil-anthropic spirits, bestowing a magnanimous commission of one hundred thousand dollars on the principals, Dancer and Macklin, as a reward. The mining men also offered to build a new school or church for the town of Raindance. But the city fathers, citing a shortage of children and an excess of sinners in the little community, expressed a greater need, convincing the affable benefactors to finance construction of a new town jail instead.

Dancer wanted Macklin to keep the entire hundred thou-sand, but the rancher would not hear of it. They argued the division of the reward for days, Dancer finally agreeing to accept one-fourth. He then sent the bulk of his portion home to his partner and uncle, John Dancer. He retained enough to buy gifts for the entire Ute band of Four Feathers, Many Ponies and Fire Cloud—blankets, knives, iron pots, tobacco, beads, hats, needles and a dozen head of fine horse breeding stock, driven to Raindance from his ranch on the Gunnison.

Colorado had been admitted to the Union as the 38th state on August 1, 1876. Territorial Governor John L. Routt stayed on, elected the first Governor of the "Centennial State." Changes were imminent, but civilization does not arrive in harness with legislation as a matter of course. A decade later, Colorado remained a rugged frontier, unsettled as a tumbleweed, mustang wild, not yet ready for the rein.

The Macklins had gone.

Days and weeks lengthened into months. Dancer's wound

no longer plagued him. He was hale and fit again, but still he lingered in Raindance. He was restless and discontent. He should get back home, get on with his life. He took long rides in the mountains on the big blood bay, visiting with the Indians, returning to the Flying M, to the trapper's shack where he had recuperated from the wounds inflicted upon him by Stone Wolf, to the cave in the mountainside where he had first seen Linda Macklin.

The winter snows had melted, the weather was perfect for travel. Why was he still here? Jack did not know. He knew only that he carried the nagging impression of something left undone—an ache for which he could find no healing balm.

One morning Dancer awoke to a beautiful, cloudless day, the blue sky artfully stitched with long lines of calling geese and ducks winging north. The air was clear and fresh and a slight breeze blew off the white mountain crests to the north, carrying a metallic crispness. Sounds of the awakening village intruded through Dancer's open window—the raspy growl of a saw on wood, empty bottles clanking onto the trash heap behind the Golconda, the jangle of trace chains, dogs yelping, the resonant ring of a heavy hammer on an anvil, a woman's shrewishly shrill admonitions and the grumbling retort of her harassed mate, and children fussing. Jack's bare feet hit the wood floor and he crossed rapidly to the bureau. He pulled open a drawer and began to throw his possibles into a travel bag.

Jack Dancer was going home.

He climbed from the valley to look down on the cluster of unremarkable structures below. The sun rising over the crest of the mountains behind the town bathed the streets in blood red and yellow-gold, fitting colors for the reckoning that had occurred there. With conflicting emotions, Dancer said his good-byes to Raindance.

The blood bay champed nervously at the bit, anxious to

be away. Jack turned and flicked the reins, giving the big horse leave to move ahead. He did not look back.

He forged steadily upward to ride the high trails and to escape the crush of men and memories. As he traveled, the wild country began to work its wonders. His hungry spirit embraced the sights and smells and sounds. Tension fled as his senses became attuned to the world around him.

Dancer paused at dusk to fish his supper from a deep pool beneath cascading falls. He broiled the sleek, speckled trout, plump with roe, over a slow fire with a piece of bacon in the cavity for seasoning. He washed down his meal with a pot of scalding coffee, rolled and smoked a cigarette, then put out the fire and moved on down the trail to seek a night camp. Through years of protecting his scalp, Jack had learned never to spend the night in the vicinity of his cookfire, as the sight and scent of the smoke was a magnet to the hostile and the curious. Nor did he make it a practice to camp too near a source of water. He did not wish to deter creatures of the wild from exercising their rights to a cool drink, and he wanted no thirsty traveler stumbling into his camp.

Just shy of noon the following day, Dancer was halted by the tattoo of onrushing hoofbeats on the trail behind him. He slipped the thong off the hammer of the sixgun in his holster and turned the horse to face the unseen rider who was advancing rapidly up the slope. His rifle lay casually across the bow of his saddle, unthreatening, but readily available.

"Hao, my brother." The Indian boy brought the piebald pony to a sudden, prancing halt.

"Well, howdy there, Fire Cloud. You ride that mustang like a real warrior, boy. Must be your leg doesn't bother you much anymore, huh?"

"There is a slight limp that I will always carry. It is nothing. My uneven step will remind me that I cannot fly like the hawk from high places."

Dancer chuckled with the grinning Ute youth.

"It will remind me, too, of my blood brother, my good friend Dancer, who saved my life," the boy said. "My heart is heavy to see you go. I have brought a gift to protect you on your journey."

Fire Cloud reached into a rawhide pouch that hung from his neck and withdrew a talisman made from the claws of a cougar and the canine teeth of a bear. He placed the necklace across the palms of both hands and extended it with ritual respect to the white man. Dancer accepted the token.

"It is good, Fire Cloud. The claws of the great cat will give me stealth and quickness. The teeth of the grizzly will fill me with strength and courage. It is a fine gift from a good friend."

Jack placed the talisman around his neck with ceremonial solemnity. "I shall wear it with pride . . .

"My heart is also heavy that I must leave the land of the Ute, and of my brother, Fire Cloud. But my spirit longs for the land to the west that is my home, the land of the Gunnison. You must come visit me there, little brother. You will always be welcome in my lodge."

They visited awhile, then the boy headed down the trail, back to his village. Dancer once again directed his vision toward home.

A whicker started in the bay's throat as its ears shot up and forward. Dancer reined the horse to a halt as they entered the clearing. The hairs at the back of his neck bristled.

Jack's eyes searched the edge of the timber surrounding the open area, halting at a hint of movement deep in the trees directly ahead. He sat without moving, a reassuring palm pressed against the neck of his mount to quiet it.

Stone Wolf walked purposefully into view, trailing the appaloosa stallion by the reins in his left hand. He stopped. The two men stared at each other, unblinking and with equal menace. The Indian was the first to break the silence.

"You cannot go. There is that between us that we must settle. Only one will leave this place."

"I know, and I understand," Dancer said, fingering the talisman at his throat. "I figured you would show. I was counting on it."

With a movement more rapid than the space of a heart-
beat, Stone Wolf dropped the reins of the spotted stallion
and crouched to his knees, training the sinister eye of his
rifle on Dancer's breast. The sudden movement startled the
bay, causing it to rear on its hind legs. The bullet from the
half-breed's gun caught the big horse in the throat, sending
it crashing down and hurling its rider aside. Dancer rolled as
he hit the ground, barely escaping being pinned beneath the
screaming, thrashing animal. He came up shooting as Stone
Wolf scampered behind a hummock of earth. Jack dove for
the cover of the still-twitching breastwork of the downed
bay's carcass.

The combatants exchanged a series of pot shots with little effect, each relatively safe in his present protected position. The day dragged on. The battle sagged.

As the sun scaled the towering evergreens that ringed the
field of battle and soared higher overhead, the day grew
increasingly warm, boring down on the men in their huddled
positions. Dancer sneaked a cautious hand to reel in his canteen, attached by rawhide ties below the pommel of his new
Denver saddle on the back of the dead bay. He took a long,
welcome pull of the cool spring water from the mouth of the
canteen, then filled a palm and bathed his face. He rolled and
lit a smoke. He checked his pistols for the fourth time since
firing his last shot.

The silence of the forest was unbroken except for the
monotonous drone of the insects that tended their tiny bug
chores, unmindful of the tense war of waiting being waged
by human intruders.

"Stone Wolf . . ."

"I am here."

"Appears to me we've got us a standoff here. I can't get to you without buying lead. But you are not about to catch me unaware, either. This fracas could take a mighty long while."

Jack was peering around the rump of the dead horse. He spied his appaloosa cropping grass at the edge of the clearing, dragging its reins, thirty yards back of the halfbreed's position.

"I have nothing more important to do. I can wait."

"Mister, you can wait until the buffalo come back if you want to, but I hope you don't mind if I go on ahead without you."

Dancer stuck a thumb and forefinger to his lips and split the quiet of the clearing with a shrill whistle. The appaloosa jerked its big head skyward and with a joyous whinny ran eagerly toward its hidden master at a canter.

Stone Wolf wheeled at the pounding of hooves behind him and threw his rifle to his shoulder to shoot the horse. Dancer stood and fired.

The .44 slug from Dancer's sixshooter struck the mechanism of the Indian's rifle and ricocheted like an enraged hornet, tearing through Stone Wolf's forearm and sending the shattered long gun clattering across the grass.

Dancer rushed forward as Stone Wolf broke for cover in a stumbling, three-pointed lope. He threw two shots in front of his fleeing adversary, halting his flight. The frantic Indian turned to look into cold brown eyes. Dancer leathered his pistol.

"You're wearing a sidearm, killer. You can try me, or I'll take you in to hang. Your choice."

"I am hurt. It is not much of a choice."

"It's the one you've got."

Stone Wolf went for his gun.

* * *

The sutler checked the crumpled list in his hand, then piled the last of the supplies onto the counter. He reached to rake in the pair of gold coins that the stranger had laid there. He wiped his hands on the front of his apron and walked to look through the open door toward the hitch rail.

"That's a mighty fine looking spotted horse you got there, mister," he said over his shoulder. "Where'd you come by him?"

"Took it off a dead Indian."

Author's Note

I have always loved the West, with its majesty and its grandeur, with its green, lush forests upon mountains that reach beyond the clouds, and wild rivers that run free and clear. And I love to read about the myths and legends of the Old West, and of its history—often more incredible than the fanciful tales it has inspired.

To appreciate the sincerity of this story and the intense, violent natures of the passionate, volatile characters portrayed on these pages, it will be beneficial to understand the personality and vitality of the land at the time it occurred, and to be aware of previous forces and events that shaped its lusty reputation.

The chaos that reigned in the tumultuous years that followed the Civil War spawned a breed of man that was to add a new and colorful chapter of explosive violence, bravery, bluster and bravado to the history of the American West— the *gunfighter*. With the nineteenth century nearing its final quarter, law and order had not kept pace with the waves of expansion and settlement. It was to this lawless milieu they came—rootless, reckless floaters and movers; brash young men and battle–scarred veterans, imperturbable and fearless as a lot.

The label of gunfighter was applied to law dogs and desperadoes alike. In a face–off on a dusty street, it mattered not which side of the badge they represented, for the ultimate law was the gun.

The habitat of the gunfighter was the rustic frontier town, begat by cattle, railroad or mining; turbid, roistering settlements crowded with saloons, dance halls and brothels; where whiskey, money and revelry all flowed freely—and were the flints that sparked the tempers of the men with tied–down guns.

There existed a blurred line between lawman and renegade, and it sometimes took first–hand knowledge to separate one from another, for they had much in common. Many gunfighters worked both sides of that line at one time or another. The guns by which these men lived and died gave them a shared identity—a membership in a distinct fraternity of the still raw West. The famous: Bat Masterson, Wyatt Earp, Luke Short, Wild Bill Hickok. The infamous: Clay Allison, Doc Holliday, Ben Thompson, John Wesley Hardin. Those lesser known, but equally deadly: Turkey Creek Jack Johnson, Jack Bridges, Temple Houston (lawyer son of Texas patriot Sam Houston), Ned Christie, Heck Thomas, Charlie Siringo and my own great-grandfather, Garland Vincent, who is thought to have killed twenty men, as a soldier and as a lawman.

There were good men and true among the gunfighters, but there was a sub-species as well, who embarked on bloody careers. Circumstances of time and place contributed to the breed. Many were disgruntled Southerners whose bitterness over their lost cause or their disenfranchisement by carpetbaggers after the war shaped them into predators on society, murdering out of sudden impulse. Some were remorseless men, contemptuous of those who did not possess their deadly skills—loners, whose egos swelled in direct proportion to their gunplay credits, their motives explainable only in their own dark minds. They acted out their private furies with a lack of constraint, seething with hatreds that they, themselves, often could not define.

The War Between The States was a grief remembered, but for most Americans, the wounds of that war became less painful and its losses were mourned with diminishing bitterness as all eyes turned westward to a great and wide land of opportunity.

In spite of Indian threat, a flood of settlers and fortune seekers poured into those open lands, the flow increasing rapidly after 1870 with the construction of the railroads. The white man had come to stay. Still, for the most part, the West of that day remained an untamed and predatory country besieged by roving bands of bandits and renegade Indians—and in the mining towns and settlements, by gamblers, camp followers, quick buck artists, bible–thumpers and rowdies.

Thus was born the temperament of this hostile and beautiful land. The West was a wild, ribald, boisterous infant, plundered by ravenous men seeking riches and power, sacrificing herself on the altar of progress, part victim and part predator, growing toward greatness.

The tale I have told you here is true to the conditions and character of the country and its inhabitants as they existed during the period in which it takes place, the final quarter of the nineteenth century.

The principals in my story are composites, incorporating the nature and character of those thousands of men and women, good and evil, who were instrumental in the making of the American West—enriching our heritage, defining our goals. Without their fervor, daring and grit, the flag of our nation would no doubt be less spangled with stars.